The Halls of Erinyel

Her First Knight, Volume 7

Ash Gray

Published by Ash Gray, 2022.

THE HALLS OF ERINYEL

First edition. November 15, 2022.

ISBN: 979-8224374793

Written by Ash Gray.

Chapter 1

The ship they booked passage on was called the *Primrose*. It was a merchant ship bound for the port at Hadun on the eastern shore. Hadun itself was outside the seven realms and was a trade port to boot, and given that it was so heavily protected by a quite formidable army, the place was virtually untouchable. Both sides of the war's conflict left it well alone, only approaching to trade for supplies, and as a result, Hadun was thriving due to Bjorn's conquest.

But Hadun had become neutral territory not simply due to its army and its value as a trading hub. Legend had it that Hadun, being on the edge of Elloris, was the very last place the ancient elves had been seen alive before their sudden disappearance. They had come to the human city in droves during their exodus, and magickal beings that they were, their mere presence had left an indelible mark on the land. It was widely believed that anyone who drew blood in Hadun would suffer a terrible curse, and so, because many took the legends of the elves quite seriously, no one ever drew blood inside the walls of Hadun.

It only took one week to cross the little patch of sea flowing between Adwean and Hadun, and when they had stepped off the ship on the eastern shore, spring had arrived. The snow had melted to slush, and the first hints of green were peeping from the ground and from the trees.

Liadan was relieved. She hated the winter, hated being cold, hated watching the trees die, but the rebirth in the spring was so marvelous, she sometimes thought the cold and suffering was worth it. Still, she understood completely why dragons slept in the winter. The beasts would be stirring now, and it was quite likely that Ava's egg would hatch as well. Back in Wildoras, dragons always hatched in the spring. Like big scaly chickens, Liadan thought with a private smile.

Hadun, being a trade hub, was a massive city, its endless rows of rooftops and chimneys spreading away to the horizon. They led their horses by the reins from the boardwalk, and as they blended into the milling crowds, the mighty battlements of the city walls cast their shadow over them. Here, there were seven temples, each one built in honor of the seven New Gods, and – to Liadan's surprise – there was even a great stone temple to the goddess Himara, an Old God and mother goddess to the women of Wildoras.

Fionn gasped when she saw the temple to Himara. "Blasphemy!" she cried in amazement as they passed beneath its shadow.

"Why is it blasphemy?" Liadan calmly inquired.

Fionn shook her head. "Why, because the Old Gods have abandoned us."

Liadan frowned. "They most certainly have not."

Fionn stared at Liadan in amazement, as if she had never quite looked at her before. "Why, Knight Liadan! I thought you were a convert, not a heathen! You did wed most readily under the blessing of Eyslath!"

"Call not my wife a heathen!" Ava commanded, strangely irate.

Fionn was walking beside Ethne as the Knight of the Sparrow led her horse on foot, and the priestess shrank under Ava's offended gaze, looking quite humbled and meek. It reminded Liadan of Lysa when she was frightened her betrayal had ruined her friendship with Ava. Fionn seemed likewise afraid of losing Ava's favor.

"My s-sweet princess," Fionn stammered, "I meant no offense!"

"And there is none taken," returned Ava sharply, "for you still have your head."

Fionn goggled at Ava, for it was unlike her to issue threats, and Liadan saw the others also look around at the princess in wonder.

The group halted as the crowds continued to press around them, and everyone watched as Fionn fell to her knees before Ava and kissed her little slippers. Lysa actually rolled her eyes in great irritation, which Liadan found interesting given that Lysa had so often groveled before Ava in a similar manner, if not less dramatic.

"Cast me not from your sight, my sweet, sweet princess!" Fionn begged, head down.

Standing beside Saoirse with her hammer and shield on her back, Rowan laughed. "Ava's pussy must be something else for all of this groveling," she said, clutching the reins of her big stallion as it loomed beside her. She eyed Lysa as she spoke, as if she had been thinking along the same lines as Liadan, and Liadan saw Lysa blush brightly.

While Rowan was smirking and amused, Liadan thought Saoirse pitied Fionn. The Knight of the Lion gazed down at Fionn almost sadly. Fionn was still on her knees and was trembling, and Liadan knew why: if Ava cast Fionn out, she would be forced to wander the world alone, living on the kindness and charity of those few who took pity on her. It would have been a lonely existence, though her blessing from Eyslath would have protected her from real danger.

Ava blushed with shame and waved a dismissive little hand, her wedding band flashing prettily in the sunlight. "Do get up, Fionn! Don't make a fool of yourself."

Still trembling, Fionn got to her feet and dusted her red robes off. She kept her head down and didn't look at anyone. Her little cheeks were bright red.

They continued walking on foot, guiding their horses on, and Liadan noticed how the others kept glancing curiously at Ava. Lysa in particular was astounded. Rowan – as ever—was amused. Saoirse just looked tired. Ethne was busy staring at Lysa's backside in her tight trousers and wasn't paying attention one way or the other.

"What has gotten into you, Ava?" demanded Lysa. She walked near Liadan and Ava and was guiding her little black mare along by the reins beside her.

"I have," said Liadan, and she heard Rowan laugh from the front of their procession. Liadan was walking beside Ava as she led their chestnut forward by the reins, and she reached over and put an arm around Ava's waist, smoothing her hand over Ava's great belly.

"My child has filled Ava with her fire," said Liadan proudly. "She shall be a mighty warrior and reclaim the birthright of all women everywhere!" So saying, Liadan kissed Ava hard on the cheek and felt her wife's skin grow hot with a blush.

"That is how I know the Old Gods have not forsaken us," Liadan gently told Fionn.

Fionn nodded. "If faith gives thee comfort, who am I to question it, Knight Liadan?"

"There's no need to question it, Fionn," said Ethne beside her. "We all know Liadan is a filthy sinner."

Chuckling rose from the group as they continued along through the sunlight and chattering crowds, and Liadan was glad to see everyone relaxed and at ease again.

The group decided to purchase supplies at the market, then rent a room at an inn for the night. It was the last warm bed they would know for quite some time, for on the other side of Hadun were the forests of Elloris, and deep within those forests were the ancient ruins of the elves, dark places, where dragons and orcs and goblins lurked. There were even tales of giant spiders, ghosts, and ogres. It was a dangerous place to raise a child, but Liadan knew that lingering in the seven realms was even more dangerous. She would rather fight orcs than watch helplessly as a guardsman's sword was plunged through Ava's pregnant belly.

At one point, Ethne said what they were all thinking and suggested they stay in Hadun. There were plenty of temples where Ava could give birth, she reasoned, and the city was the safest in the land at the moment.

Though Liadan liked the idea of staying in Hadun, she reminded Ethne that Ava's pregnancy must be kept secret as much as was possible. If Ava were to give birth in such a large and busy city as Hadun, the news would spread like wildfire, and before long, King Eyvor's men would be kicking in their door.

And there was also the fact that Fionn would not be welcome inside a temple. Mother Tiede, in bitterness and anger, would have already sent the ravens out informing the other temples of a rogue priestess who was now "impure."

They could always return to Hadun for supplies but depending on how far into the forest they went, the return trek could be quite long. Liadan feared they had been followed or that King Eyvor had already learned of Ava's pregnancy, and it was her intention to stay hidden in the forest until her firstborn was quite grown and capable of defending herself.

Thankfully, Wildoras children grew supernaturally fast. The thought occurred to Liadan as they were shopping in the market, and as the others watched in amusement, she purchased a great deal of fabric to make clothes for their child, bought cloths for swaddling, bought blankets, and even bought Ava a new green traveling gown, which Ava squealed over in girlish delight.

By the time they were leaving the market, Laidan and Ava's chestnut was loaded down with Liadan's purchases, and Ava kept bouncing up on tiptoe to kiss Liadan and praise her as her strong provider.

Privately, Liadan didn't feel pleased by Ava's praise, for it was technically Ava's gold they were spending, for it was the same gold that had been taken from Queen Saraid's tomb, and only a little of it was truly Liadan's. But since Liadan had already spent so much of her own gold on the journey, she welcomed Ava's kisses and pink-cheeked glee.

"And one day when I have my crown again," Ava said, taking Liadan's hand, "I shall provide for you! We shall have our cozy bed chamber again, my love. I swear it!"

Ava had sounded so determined that Liadan didn't doubt it, and she thought back to what Ceana had said in Hastow: no woman of House Damaris with a spine would turn her back on her own legacy.

As if Liadan's thought had summoned her, Ceana appeared in the market crowds, watching Liadan from a distance. She was wearing her silver engraved armor with the red cape, and her expression was solemn. Liadan halted in her tracks and stared. Ceana grimly stared back. The others were talking and laughing and hadn't noticed Ceana or the fact that Liadan stood frozen, except for Ava, who drew near and said in a low, fearful voice, "What is it, my knight?"

Ava hugged Liadan's arm and glanced around, but she didn't appear to notice Ceana.

"Can't you see her?" Liadan said in confusion. "Ceana! My sister is right . . ." Liadan's voice trailed away, for Ceana had vanished.

Ava frowned. "You must be tired. Fionn said we should have let you rest longer, that the effects of her spell might make you delirious, but we had to make haste from Adwean—"

"Then maybe Fionn shouldn't have fucked Liadan so many times," joked Ethne, drawing near. She had heard only Ava's words and seemed unaware of the discussion about Ceana. She was flushed and happy, and Lysa was hugging her arm and looking just as happy. Behind them, Fionn watched them bitterly.

Noticing Liadan's distress, Ethne frowned. "What's the matter, good Liadan? You look as if . . . Well, not to sound cliched, but you look as if you'd seen a ghost."

"Perchance I have," said Liadan heavily, but since Ceana had quite vanished, she turned away and decided to say nothing of it. The others were watching her with concern, and she didn't want to upset anyone.

"Come," she said, "let us find an inn for the night. Perhaps you are right, my Ava. Perhaps I need rest."

They rented a room at an inn called Himara's Rest. As the sun set outside the window, the knights stripped their armor and everyone prepared for bed – everyone except Liadan, who volunteered for first watch. Once the others were sleeping and a good fire was roaring on the hearth, Liadan went to the window and went still: Ceana was down in the street, gazing up at her.

Liadan knew this time that she hadn't been hallucinating. Her sister was down in the street, staring at her! It would have been easy for Ceana to have followed them from Hastow, especially since one of the priestesses would have healed her after she took Saoirse's arrow to the shoulder. But why? Why follow them all the way across the sea?

Ceana nodded at Liadan, beckoning her to come down. Her expression was grim, but her eyes were urgent.

Liadan hesitated, gazing down at her sister. Was it a trap? Had Ceana led a horde of temple knights to the city to slay them? Would Ceana do that?

Liadan knew Ceana did not approve of her match with Ava and was jealous of her friendship with Ethne as well. Back in Hastow, Liadan had leapt to Ethne's defense without blinking, had been willing to slay her own sister to keep Ethne safe. Ceana would have been deeply hurt by that. Perhaps she had come seeking revenge. Would she have taken the opportunity to sabotage them? She knew of their plans to head to Elloris. She could have very easily told Mother Tiede that she would hunt down and slay Fionn, only to come after Liadan instead.

Deciding she would take the risk, Liadan quietly left the room and went downstairs. Outside, the last chilly wisps of winter wind were howling through the dark streets, and the streets were lined with glowing braziers, their fires leaping against the cold.

Ceana waited across the street from the inn, standing in the shadow of a shop that had closed. When she saw Liadan emerge, she beckoned with another gesture and turned, walking down the alley behind the shop. Liadan followed.

"Ceana?" Liadan said when she had caught up to her sister.

They came to a barren yard behind the shop, where mud and snow were slush on the ground, and a well stood under the open sky, its bucket dangling. Ceana went to the well and leaned her back against it. She folded her arms, simply gazing at Liadan. The moonlight gleamed on her silver armor, shone upon her long red hair, which hung loose behind her shoulders.

Liadan uncertainly drew near. "Why have you followed me all the way here? You crossed the sea just for me?"

"Aye," said Ceana heavily. "I tried to catch you in Adwean, but you were injured, and then you left so quickly. I wished to say fare thee well, and to send a raven would have been too great a risk. It would have given away your position."

Liadan frowned. "What do you mean?"

"I was expelled from the temple for failing in my duty," said Ceana.

"Gods be good," sighed Liadan apologetically. "I never should have come to Hastow. I have caused you so much grief—"

Ceana held up a gauntlet and smiled. "It is so like you blame yourself, but in truth, the fault lies with no one. Mother Tiede has always lusted for Fionn. She was jealous that Fionn chose your friend, is all." She blinked angrily for a moment, and Liadan suspected that Ceana *also* was envious that Fionn had chosen Ethne.

"My expulsion from the temple was merely an excuse to vent her rage," went on Ceana. "Mother Tiede is furious that Fionn has escaped her. She shall send other knights after you, and indeed, they have already crossed the sea in your wake and are even now in the city. You have been warned."

Liadan felt her soul sinking in her body. "As if we didn't have enough to deal with," she said wearily. "Thank you for the warning, my sister. And . . . I am sorry for . . ."

"Siding with your friend?" said Ceana with a sad smile. "Do not be sorry, dear Liadan. You and I were close back in Wildoras, but that was a long time ago, and we have drifted apart. Again, the fault lies with no one. It is the way of things. I shall always be your sister and I shall always love you. That is what matters."

Liadan smiled, relieved. She looked up as a thought occurred to her. "Why don't you travel with us?"

Ceana hesitated. "Liadan . . ."

Liadan stepped forward. "There is no reason you should travel alone! You are my family, and if I have the means to take care of you, then I should. Look at this!" Liadan reached inside her cloak and pulled out her coin purse, which was quite fat and heavy. She held it open, and Ceana looked inside, lifting her brows in surprise at the contents.

"We found a small fortune while hiding in the Valley of the Queens," Liadan explained. "I could give you a purse, and you would be set for many years, but you would still be alone. Won't you come with me instead and we could share it?"

Ceana hesitated again. Her eyes were full of guilt.

"If you are worried about Ava . . ." Liadan began.

Ceana smiled. "No. I am not worried about your pretty, featherbrained princess," she teased, and Liadan smiled as well.

"No," said Ceana, serious now, and she glanced uneasily around, as if she feared someone were watching. "I am more worried about Fionn and your dog friend. It is not my wish to watch as they carry on. I suffered enough while serving at the temple."

Liadan laughed. "Oh, that. I don't think Fionn desires Ethne any longer. She is more fascinated with Ava and myself, but only, I suspect, because her fate is in our hands. We are the unspoken leaders of this little venture. She does not wish to be cast out."

Ceana laughed tonelessly. "She is clever, using her womanly wiles to seduce you and Ava to her sympathies. I confess, I do not wish to witness that either, little sister."

Liadan laughed yet again. "Then we shall not lay with Fionn, if it pleases you." She stepped close and said seriously, "You are my sister and I love you. I would not have you wander the world alone when you needn't. Come with me into Elloris. We will raise my child together and be close like we were in times past." She held out her hand and waited.

Ceana hesitated yet again. Then her eyes relented, and she took Liadan's hand. They gripped each other's forearms and pulled into a one-armed hug, and laughing, they returned together to the inn . . . Liadan never dreaming that they were, indeed, being watched.

FIONN COULDN'T SLEEP. She lay in the bed beside Ava, in the room they had rented at the inn, as the fire crackled on the hearth, as the soft breathing of the sleeping knights rose on the air, and she tried not to think of the temple and all she had lost by laying with Ethne. And in the end, Ethne hadn't even loved her! Had lying with the Sparrow Knight even been worth it? Fionn had looked in Ethne's pretty gray eyes as they were making love, and she had fallen head over heels, but the Knight of the Sparrow did not feel the same. No, Ethne only had eyes for Lysa.

Fionn chided herself that she should have seen it coming. After all, Ethne had been weeping rather pathetically about Lysa when she met her in the chapel. Why wouldn't she go crawling back the moment Lysa batted her lashes? And though Fionn knew she had walked right into it, she still felt cheated, and she gazed upon Ethne and Lysa's love with hatred from afar. Even now, they were snuggled in the bed on the other side of Ava, so happy and smiling. Ethne was in nothing but her underarmor and her muscular arms bulged as she held Lysa, who was sleeping against her shoulder.

What did Ethne see in Lysa? Fionn couldn't fathom it. Lysa wasn't very pretty, and she was rude and mocking, always calling Ethne a dog and bedding other women! From the chatter Fionn had overheard, Lysa was right awful. The only appealing thing about her was her wild spirit – *that* the knights couldn't get enough of, and they talked incessantly about what a "little dragon" Lysa was in bed, dominating these big, strong knights and riding them and tasting them. Even Ethne, bickering constantly with Lysa as she did, was submissive to her in bed.

And Fionn had to admit, she found Lysa's untamed nature as desirable as everyone else did. She enjoyed watching Lysa ride, watching Lysa practice with her sword, watching Lysa finally dominated by Saoirse, the one woman she could not dominate herself. Fionn had watched Saoirse plow Lysa over the table and had wet her smallclothes wanting to plow Lysa herself.

Regardless of all of that, Fionn still felt she was the better woman for Ethne. Fionn knew she was sweet and kind and gentle, she was honest and true, and whenever Ethne was hurt, she also had the power to heal her! Lysa could do none of that! If anything, Lysa was the reason Ethne was always getting hurt!

Pushing away angry thoughts of Lysa, Fionn nuzzled her cheek in the pillow and tried to sleep. She suspected it was the last time in a long while that she would feel a proper pillow under her head. She was just drifting off when the door opened, and in came Liadan and Ceana!

Fionn's mouth fell open. As the knights tromped into the room with jingling armor and sat at the table under the window, Fionn closed her eyes and pretended to sleep. She had to resist the urge to bounce up and run to Ceana. She had missed the red-haired knight more than she was willing to confess, but she wanted to eavesdrop. She wanted to know why Ceana was there.

". . . long journey ahead," Liadan was saying wearily. "I wish there was more room for you in the bed."

"I'd sooner slit my own wrists than sleep in that bed near Ethne," said Ceana with a flat laugh.

Liadan laughed as well. Fionn noticed the Knight of the Wild was always smiling and laughing a great deal when around her sister. She thought it sweet that Liadan doted on Ceana so greatly, yet Ceana – for all her jealousy of Ethne – didn't seem to see it.

"We could both sleep on the floor near Saoirse and Rowan. It is warmer there, anyway, by the fire," Liadan said.

"Those two have always been inseparable, haven't they?" said Ceana, who was staring at Saoirse and Rowan where they lay near the hearth. The women had pushed their bedrolls together, and Saoirse was holding Rowan in her arms, while Rowan's cheek was pressed against the Lion's shoulder and she was smiling in her sleep, happy to be held by her love.

"The gods have mercy on them and me," Ceana said, still staring at the newlyweds on the floor.

Liadan frowned. "What was that, dear sister?"

Ceana stirred herself. "Nothing. How is married life treating you thus far?" she asked to change the subject. The jingle of armor.

Fionn opened her eyes the tiniest bit and saw that Ceana was removing her gauntlets. She laid them on the table and was watching as Liadan poured ale into two tankards from a pitcher. Ceana took one and drank, and Fionn had to resist the urge to gasp: temple knights were not supposed to drink!

"It has treated me just fine," Liadan answered, gazing toward Ava where the princess lay sleeping on the bed. "Ava is a good woman, as you shall soon learn, and we shall have many fine, strong daughters."

Liadan wasn't aware of it, but Ceana was gazing at her sister sadly and almost with pity. She didn't speak on it, however, and instead took a gulp from her tankard.

"And you shall rule the seven realms forever and forever," sang Ceana tonelessly, as if finishing something tiresome she had heard over and over.

Liadan grinned. "Yes, we shall," she said and raised her tankard. "Here's to Isliine!"

Ceana raised her tankard as well, and after smiling at each other, they both drank deeply.

Ceana swallowed and set her tankard on the table. "But tell me true," she said, and her eyes went to Fionn, who stiffened and quickly closed her eyes. "Fionn has no romantic inkling toward you or Ava?"

"None," said Liadan with a laugh. "I have told you, she manipulates us to stay in our good graces. She did give Ava a speech about how easily she could survive on her own, but it was only to make Ava pity her and beg her to stay."

"And it worked," said Ceana, amused.

Fionn held down a blush. It was entirely true: she had told Ava that she was leaving to be on her own, had made a big fuss about being hurt by Ethne – which she truly was – in the hope that Ava would take pity and ask her to stay with them. She felt bad for manipulating the princess, but her survival depended on Ava liking her. She knew that now. Perhaps with Ceana there, she would no longer need Ava's friendship. Perhaps Ceana had come to take her back to the temple. Had she been forgiven then? Bright hope blossomed in her chest.

Liadan tipped back her tankard and finished the last of her ale. "I shall step downstairs for another helping of the house stew," she said, setting down her tankard. "Keep watch in my wake?"

"Aye," said Ceana with a laugh. "That you would take advantage of my presence for stew – I see you haven't changed."

Liadan grinned – such a rare phenomenon that Fionn nearly opened her eyes all the way in amazement -—and rose from her seat. She clapped Ceana happily on the shoulder as she passed and went quietly out the door, closing it behind her.

"I know you are awake, little eavesdropper," said Ceana when Liadan had gone, and she tipped back her tankard for another gulp.

Embarrassed, Fionn slowly sat up, pushing her mass of blonde hair back from her face. "How long did you know?" she asked, rising meekly from the bed.

"The moment I saw you," said Ceana, gesturing. "Come to me," she said quietly. "I have missed thee greatly."

Fionn's heart was pounding in her ears and butterflies were in her stomach. She felt like a silly girl, but she was pleased to know that Ceana had missed her. She crossed the room to the knight, who was watching her intently, her blue eyes, so like Liadan's, filled with softness and affection.

Fionn felt shy under Ceana's doting gaze and fanned her pale lashes down as she finally stood before her. Her heart leapt when Ceana took her by the waist and lifted her easily onto her lap. Then the knight took another drink of ale, gazing down at Fionn thoughtfully.

"M-Many years have you guarded me at the t-temple," said Fionn, flustered, "but you never before sat me on your lap!"

Ceana smiled. "We aren't at the temple. There is no one here to scold me."

"You are wrong!" Fionn said at once. "I am here! Why are you drinking? You know it violates your vows!"

"Just as spreading your thighs for Ethne violated yours," said Ceana quietly and took another drink.

Fionn blushed furiously. "How can you say such things?!"

Ceana shrugged. "It is the truth."

"Is it meant to hurt me?" Fionn asked, holding back tears.

Ceana looked down at her apologetically. "No, sweet Fionn. Please . . . do not weep."

Fionn cast her eyes down and hugged herself. "I wanted Ethne. She was so beautiful and gentle, weeping for her love. I wanted to heal her . . . It is my nature."

"And so, you did," said Ceana, "while ignoring how I have suffered these long years, wanting you."

Fionn looked at her quickly. "Have you suffered, my knight?"

"Aye," said Ceana softly, gazing down at her. Her finger touched Fionn's chin, and she peered absently into her eyes. She looked as if she would kiss Fionn, but thinking better of it, took another drink.

"Why have you come?" Fionn asked, disappointed that she hadn't been kissed. "To take me back?"

Ceana frowned. "No, sweet Fionn. I have been expelled from the temple."

Fionn gasped, covering her mouth with both little hands. "Oh, Ceana! I'm so sorry!"

"There is no returning for either of us, I fear," Ceana went on heavily. "Liadan has invited me to join your party, and I have accepted. Does that please you?"

"Y-Yes," Fionn admitted, quivering beneath Ceana's soft gaze. "Shall you be my knight and protector again?"

"I shall be whatever you doth wish, sweet Fionn," said Ceana gently.

Fionn's heart fluttered again. She looked at Ceana's lips and wanted to kiss her.

"That is," went on Ceana, "so long as you don't lay with Ethne again – or any other woman in this group of lechers," she said, her disgusted eyes scanning over the sleeping bodies of the others.

Fionn blushed to her hairline, embarrassed that Ceana knew of her deeds. She had lain with Saoirse, Ava, Liadan, Lysa, *and* Ethne. And Ceana knew. Gods have mercy! Fionn dropped her face in her hands. She felt Ceana stroking her hair.

"Why are you ashamed?" Ceana said soothingly. "I care not that you have lain with these women, but if you do so again, I may have to strike them down. I have nothing to lose now. I would do so gladly."

"Oh!" Fionn cried, horrified. "Don't say such things! You must be kind to the others, and there mustn't be any violence among us! And you must be kind to Ava! Tis true that I have manipulated her, but I do truly like her. She is a better woman than you assume."

"So it is settled then?" said Ceana. "You shall let no other woman touch you nor taste your sweet pussy. Tis mine alone?"

Fionn blushed brightly to hear Ceana speaking to casually about her sex, but she whispered happily, "Yes. I shall let no other. And you shall promise to stop drinking and to be kind!"

"I promise," said Ceana softly, her eyes wistful as she gazed down at Fionn.

They kissed.

"Do you trust me, sweet Fionn?" Ceana whispered when they had pulled apart.

Fionn gazed up at Ceana dotingly. "Of course, I trust you, my knight!"

Ceana smiled and pinched Fionn's chin affectionately as she gazed down at her. "How it warms me that you gaze upon me so lovingly."

Fionn's lashes fluttered and she coyly looked down.

"Listen to me, Fionn," Ceana said, suddenly grim. "Tomorrow something unpleasant may happen, and you must stay at my side. No matter how it looks, it will be to our benefit."

Fionn frowned, but pushing aside her confusion, she said happily, "You have guarded my life for years. I see no reason I should not trust you completely."

Happy to hear this, Ceana leaned down, and they kissed again. Over on the bed, Ethne listened grimly.

IN THE MORNING, LIADAN was glad when the others received Ceana warmly. It was not in jolly Rowan's nature to hold grudges, and Saoirse, while reserved, was not openly rude to Ceana. Ceana in turn was her usual stoic self, though she was warmer to Liadan's friends and even kissed Ava on her cheeks in greeting, which the others found astounding.

Everyone seemed happy to have Ceana there – everyone except Ethne, who Liadan noticed several times watching Ceana with suspicion and disdain.

That morning, they guided their horses on foot to the city gate. They were heading toward the northern gate, for Ceana had insisted on it, and though the eastern gate was more ideal, Liadan trusted her sister's counsel and obeyed.

It was a bright, cold day, and the streets were crowded as usual. Fionn walked beside Ceana as the knight guided her horse on foot, and the two seemed happy in each other's company, speaking in low voices and smiling. Ethne watched them darkly for a time, then led her horse forward to walk beside Liadan, who had been walking with Ava a little way ahead of her.

"What in hell is Ceana doing here?" Ethne demanded without preamble. She was speaking low so that Ceana and Fionn would not overhear, and her slanted eyes glared hatred at their backs.

Liadan had been speaking to Ava and both looked around to find the Sparrow Knight gazing at them crossly.

"I thought you'd be thrilled," said Liadan. "She has taken Fionn off your hands, has she not? Fionn is so distracted, she has not thought to slap you for your vile use of her – not that she would."

Ethne scowled. "I should be thrilled that the same woman who did try to slay me barely the week before shall now ride at my back and watch me sleep at night?"

"Who hasn't tried to slay you?" Liadan playfully returned.

"Well, aren't you in a merry mood," said Ethne irritably. "Listen to me, Liadan! Something is terribly wrong here! I know you don't want to hear it, but your sister hasn't come all the way across the sea just for thee—"

"Oh, Ethne!" cried Ava in exasperation. "I grow weary of all the suspicion and bickering among you knights! Ceana was upholding her sworn duty as a knight of Eyslath's temple. That is why she was forced to attack thee!"

Ethne snorted. "Forced, my arse. She wanted me dead and still does! And you're the last one who should defend her, Ava. She hath never approved of your match, nor doth she now. She only pretends to so that Liadan will aid her. She despises you, princess."

Ava looked unhappy to hear Ethne's words. Large with child, she was sitting astride the chestnut horse she shared with Liadan and cast her eyes down.

Walking alongside the horse, Liadan put a comforting hand on Ava's knee and frowned at Ethne. "That is not true! Ethne, cease your delusional rambling!"

Ethne looked at Liadan with pity. "Oh, wake up, the pair of you! Fionn and Ceana have both manipulated you for their own survival. While there is no doubt in my mind that they could aid us greatly in this journey, the deception is there. You would be a fool not to mark it."

Try as she might to deny it, Ethne's words had placed a seed of doubt in Liadan's mind. She wanted to trust and believe in Ceana, but if Liadan was honest with herself, Ceana wasn't the same person she remembered. They had grown apart, and perhaps there would be no rectifying it.

They passed through the northern gate and emerged at last on the edge of the forest. It was known as Wildhold, Liadan knew. Its trees were gigantic, with vast trunks that could house an entire family within, and warm green tops that could rival small mountains in height. But Liadan didn't have time to marvel at the beauty of the forest ahead, for blocking her path in a line, as if they'd been waiting for her, was a row of knights in silver armor, their breastplates engraved with the rose sigil of House Damaris, and they were grimly pointing crossbows.

Chapter 2

Sitting astride the chestnut horse, Ava barely had time to register what was happening before the men fired their crossbows. Most were aimed at Saoirse and Rowan, the two of them being perceived as the greater threats, and Lysa and Ethne screamed in shock and anger as the two women went down in pools of blood. Saoirse was slain instantly, but Rowan – being half-giant – rose up again with bolts riddled in her face, roaring and screaming, and was taken down with another fired round as the others looked on in open-mouthed horror.

"NO!" Liadan bellowed, leaping forward, hand out. There was an explosion of light, and many of the men watched as their crossbows went flying from their hands and away through the air. Some of the men were blown back by the force of Liadan's magick, while others were blown into bloody pieces, collapsing in piles of meat and shredded armor where they stood. The remaining men, outraged to see their fellows felled, pulled their blades and dove forward. Lysa and Ethne, tearstained and screaming, likewise pulled their blades and engaged them.

Ava couldn't move for her shock. Clutching her dragon egg close in one trembling arm, she stared and stared at the bodies, as all around her, chaos ensued. Saoirse and Rowan's faces were riddled with bolts, and they lay there, side by side, unmoving, expressions slack. They looked as if they were sleeping, as beside them, their horses nickered wildly and bucked, adding to the chaos, nearly trampling the still bodies of their owners.

Ava's horse was also bucking. She screamed and begged it to stop, scrambled to tame it as she pulled the reins with one frantic hand, but it was useless. If she didn't dismount, she would be thrown.

"Wife!" Liadan shouted, appearing frantic beside Ava. She was bloody, having disengaged from the fight, and her face was streaked with tears. She reached up and grabbed Ava by the waist. Ava braced her small hand on Liadan's shoulder, and as the knight was lifting her down from the bucking horse, one of the men shouted, "There! Don't let her escape! Ceana, don't let the princess escape! Or our deal is forfeit!"

Ava couldn't believe it when, pushing aside a sobbing Fionn, Ceana leapt forward and punched Liadan away from Ava. Liadan grunted and lost her hold, leaving Ava to go tumbling from the horse.

Ava screamed as she fell helplessly to the ground, but by some miracle, she managed to twist around and fall on her side, sparing both dragon egg and baby from the impact. Instead, searing pain shot up her arm and she screamed softly, but she was relieved when she felt her child turning unharmed inside her, stricken with fear but unharmed, and the dragon was likewise turning in its egg. Behind her, the chestnut whinnied in terror and galloped full speed into the trees of Wildhold.

Boots stamped and dust rose around Ava as the fighting continued, as Eyvor's men continued to engage Lysa and the knights. Lysa and Ethne were fighting wildly. Ava could hear Lysa screaming in rage, and Ethne's dark brown hair had come loose of its bun as she moved past Ava, deflecting a blow when one of Eyvor's men landed a savage strike on her shield.

Liadan, meanwhile, was locked in battle with Ceana, as Fionn hovered on the edge of them, watching in shock and utter horror, her mouth open behind her small hands.

"Ceana!" Liadan gasped as the two barbarian sisters locked blades. "Why have you done this? Have you gone mad—?"

Liadan's baffled demands were cut off when Ceana sneered and kicked her sister away, forcing their blades apart. Face twisted with hatred, she extended her hand, casting a stream of golden light that Liadan quickly deflected with her shield.

"You made your choice at the temple, Liadan!" Ceana snarled. "You chose them over me! Now live with it!" So saying, she raised her blade and fell upon Liadan with brutal blow after blow, each barely deflected by Liadan, whose hands were trembling with fury. They struggled, as behind them, Fionn screamed, "Stop! Stop! You shall slay each other!"

Fionn's pleas, of course, went ignored, and the sisters continued to have at each other, completely focused on their sparring match as if they were the only ones there. When once she was baffled and sad, now Liadan was vicious, betrayed and hurt as she felt, and she used everything she had, putting her full supernatural strength behind each blow, sending flames of golden light at her sister that were so hot, Ava felt the sweat breaking out on her face long after they were extinguished.

Glaring, Liadan caught Ceana off-guard and bashed her sister quite suddenly in the face with her shield. As Ceana staggered back from the blow, Liadan plunged her sword in Ceana's side, and though her expression was cold, Ava thought she saw regret in Liadan's wet blue eyes when she ripped the flaming blade free.

Eyes wide and baffled, Ceana staggered away and dropped her flaming blade, which extinguished in the mud. She clutched her side as she collapsed on her back, where she lay coughing blood. Her silver armor had been melted by the flame of Liadan's blade, melted and peeled open like butter. The silver was dripping as surely as her blood.

"No!" Fionn wailed and lunged forward, falling to her knees beside Ceana, where she wept bitterly. "How could you!" Fionn sobbed, her shoulders shaking. She bowed her head. "Your own sister!"

"My sister," growled Liadan, "who hath slain my sisters!" So saying, she waved at the bodies of Saoirse and Rowan, who lay solemn and bloody nearby.

Still panting on her side, Ava saw Lysa's boots come pelting her way through the mud. The former handmaiden crouched beside Ava and helped her to sit up. Her voice was hoarse with tears as she said, "Come, Ava! We must away into the forest! Come! Before more of them arrive!"

Ava looked around: all her father's men lay dead. Trembling with pain from her fall, she allowed Lysa to help her stand and hissed in misery: she was pretty certain her arm was either broken or sprained. Lysa was leading her away when she realized Liadan wasn't following and looked back.

The Knight of the Wild was standing over Ceana, watching with tears in her eyes as Fionn struggled to heal her. The little priestess was praying, but the words were broken from her weeping. The spell wasn't working, and Ceana was dying. Liadan stood pale and stricken.

Ethne, bloody and panting, went to Liadan and grabbed her arm, shaking her slightly. Liadan remained transfixed with grief.

"Come, Liadan! We must away!" Ethne begged. "We must away, I beg you!"

Liadan did not move.

"We must away, my love!" Ava called, surprised by how cracked with tears her voice was.

Hearing Ava's voice, Liadan finally blinked and stirred. Still shocked and blank-eyed, she allowed Ethne to pull her around by the arm, and then they fled, the four of them, into the ancient green forest. They walked as quickly as they could, their horses having abandoned them during the fighting. Ava was in a daze of pain, and over the pulsing in her ears, she thought she heard Lysa babbling something about following the horses, which had run far ahead.

"Ava can't walk, she's hurt," Lysa said, her voice a sob. "We must find the horses!" She was helping Ava walk by supporting her with her arm, but she was so small that she could barely hold Ava up.

Feeling guilty and like a burden, Ava tried to pry herself free of Lysa. "I can walk, I can w-walk, dear Lysa—"

"No, you can't!" Lysa cried. "You fell off a horse! You're lucky you didn't miscarry!"

"Lysa—" Ava began, still protesting.

"Liadan, snap out of it! Carry your wife!" Ethne shouted.

Ava looked over: Liadan was in a daze of grief. But as if she had remembered herself, The Knight of the Wild turned and gently gathered Ava into her arms, carrying her forward.

They made better time after that, moving faster and faster through the giant, looming trees. The green canvas above was so thick that the forest was very cool and shady. The ancient trees were covered with flowers and vines, and flowers were blossoming already through the last dregs of snow. Little rabbits scattered in terror before them, disappearing into the underbrush. A snail made its slow way up a great fallen log as they passed. In the distance, a deer screamed a warning to its brethren, and there was a soft rush of rustling bushes as several deer fled at the sight of them.

Curled in Liadan's strong arms, Ava looked around and thought the forest beautiful, but she was in too much pain, and her heart was too heavy with sadness and fear to appreciate it. Saoirse and Rowan were dead and gone, just like that, and because of her father! Her father had sent those men to kill her, kill her child! Fury coursed through Ava. Fury and sadness. She looked up at Liadan, who was still blank and shocked, and blamed herself for her lover's grief. Because Ava had insisted on her pregnancy and had insisted on her crusade against Bjorn, she had made herself a target and had brought more enemies down upon them when before, King Eyvor had been content to ignore their existence entirely. Liadan, piece by piece, was losing everything and everyone that was important to her, and because of Ava's desire to take back Illa and the seven realms for women. Ava was beginning to wonder if Ceana hadn't been right about her. Perhaps she would be Liadan's downfall after all.

Lysa seemed convinced that more of Eyvor's men would come after them, but none did. She kept glancing back, biting her lip, her brown eyes large with fear. She was bloody and torn from the battle, her brown hair was mussed, and she couldn't seem to stop crying. Ava knew that Saoirse and Rowan's deaths must have hit her hard, for they had been her lovers, even for a short while.

"Do you think they shall bury them proper?" Lysa sniffed, her eyes down as the group walked on through the great trees.

Liadan continued to stare in shock and said nothing. Tears coursed down her face. She didn't look at anyone, not even Ava, who she carried. She just stared and stared into the distance. Ava gazed up at her anxiously, knowing that Liadan was more than likely wondering whether or not Ceana had lived.

Ethne didn't answer Lysa either. Because Liadan was in a shocked trance, Ethne had taken over as their leader and was walking grim-faced and cold at the front of the procession. She seemed more angry than sad about what had happened. Her lips were tight, and her eyes were burning with fury. She never glanced back for pursuing enemies, but she kept one gauntlet on her sword hilt at all times.

Ethne suddenly halted, her eyes on the ground. She took a knee and reached out. Liadan drew near to Ethne, and gazing down from Liadan's arms, Ava could see their chestnut horse lying on the muddy snow. It was dead. To her horror, one of its legs had been sawed clean off, and its backend was a mass of bloody tissue. The horse's eyes were haunted and staring. Its side was riddled with arrows.

"Poor thing," sniffed Lysa. Her face darkened. "Who would shoot it down?!" She gasped. "And its throat is slashed!"

Ethne reached up and gently closed the horse's blank, staring eyes. Liadan's saddlebags – and all her purchases from the market – were still hanging off the horse, and Ethne pulled the bags off, slinging them over her shoulder. Then she stood, her eyes still scanning the ground, and she went still when she spotted something else.

Ava followed Ethne's gaze and her heart sank to see Lysa's black mare a few feet onward. It, too, was lying in the withered grass and was riddled with arrows. The horse was bloody but still alive and nickering weakly. It kicked and kicked against the mud, as if it were trapped in a web. Standing over the mare, hands bloody, was a dark green orc.

Ava gasped. The orc must have been seven feet tall. It was a woman clad in furs, feet bare, tusks protruding from her bottom lip. Her black hair was matted and wild, and on her back was a longbow made of dragon bone and a quiver of red-feathered arrows. She had slung the leg of the chestnut horse over her shoulder, and in her other hand was a bloody hunting knife. She stood frozen, gazing at them, perhaps waiting to be attacked. She was alone and would not have survived against them, big as she was. She simply waited.

Exhausted from the encounter at the gate as all of them were, Ava was relieved when Ethne didn't seem inclined to fight either. She raised her hands in a show of peace and took a step back. The orc, seeing this, nodded grimly and did not reach for her bow.

"Come," Ethne said, turning away. "We shall find another path deeper in."

As they followed Ethne in another direction, Ava saw the orc remain very still, watching them with her beady black eyes. They had barely been in the forest twenty minutes and had already been seen. Once the orc returned to her people, she would inform them of the strangers in Wildhold, and then they would really have to remain on-guard.

After a few hours walking, they stumbled across the first ruins. The trees here were not as thick, though what trees there were had taken over the city, bursting through the ceilings and walls of the ancient buildings which mostly – amazingly enough – were still in-tact.

Ava's mouth fell open in awe, for the architecture of the ancient elves was delicate and beautiful. They stood before an endless sea of ancient white buildings whose towers and spires rose like pearly chess pieces above the great trees. Most of the buildings were made of smooth wood and white stone, and instead of the harsh angles of human architecture, they were round and soft like teardrops.

Many white statues of elves stood along the cracked pavement of the streets. They towered over the group as they passed tiny below, clutching books, carrying stone candles, standing against a false wind in flowing robes. And beyond the statues were the buildings – ancient libraries, pavilions, little bridges over streams, coliseums, quaint houses with tall glass windows, little palaces, big palaces, and then . . .

"At last," breathed Ethne. "A temple."

The temple stood at the very heart of the city ruins, large and imposing, its round and golden rooftops rising over the surrounding buildings with windows like gold-framed eyelids. It had taken them so long to reach it that the sun was setting behind it in the sky, giving its white spires a glowing shimmer in the misty dusk as they reflected the watery sunset. The front step was shaped like rippling water that had spilled forward in a white pool, and a statue stood on either side of the great, golden, arched doors. Each statue was that of an elven woman, who appeared to be holding a candle in one hand while holding a finger to her lips with the other.

"The elven goddess, Erinyel," said Ethne, gazing in awe up at the statues. "The goddess of secrets. Huh. It might have been fitting if Ava's child were still a secret." She started up the step, and the others followed, Liadan still carrying Ava close in her arms.

Ethne tried pulling open the great doors, but they were simply too heavy and too enormous. Ava watched the Sparrow Knight struggle and realized the elves had likely opened the doors with magick, just like the doors of the tombs in the Valley of Queens.

"Let Liadan try," Ava said.

Ethne glanced back over her shoulder, and Ava knew she was likely thinking that Liadan was in no condition to cast magick. The Knight of the Wild was still in shock, still in a trance, but hearing Ava, she lifted her eyes to the doors, and Ava saw Liadan's eyes glow with power. A second later, and the great doors had swung outward of their own accord.

"Thank the gods for your strange powers, Liadan," said Ethne with a weak laugh. She glanced past the others into the forest and her eyes were worried. "Come. Let us enter in and quickly. I suspect we were followed here, though by Eyvor's men or orcs, I cannot say."

The inside of the temple was almost pitch black but for the stream of pale sunlight that reached through the broken ceiling of the foyer. If not for that sunlight, they wouldn't have been able to see inside at all. Ava could see a smooth wooden floor, the panels of which she could only assume had been preserved by the spell that had been placed over Elloris. On the walls hung ancient banners of the goddess Erinyel, also miraculously preserved. The corridor beyond the foyer disappeared into darkness, and beyond the ray of sunlight there, it was impossible to see what lay ahead.

"How will entering this dusty old temple protect us?" said Lysa, who had stepped forward and was peering apprehensively inside the great yawning doors.

"You are forgetting why we came here in the first place," said Ethne. "This is hallowed ground, Lysa! Don't you recall the elven legends? No man may shed blood inside one of these places – and no woman either."

"What about monthlies?" Lysa joked, but the joke was delivered flatly, as if she were trying to enter a playful banter with Ethne but just didn't have the heart after recent events.

Ethne drew near and placed a comforting hand on Lysa's shoulder. "I will keep you safe, fair Lysa. Come." She turned away, gazing anxiously toward the forest. "Enter. Hurry!"

Lysa hesitated and stepped carefully into the foyer, moving as gingerly as if she thought the floor might have been rotten and given away beneath her. Still carrying Ava, Liadan followed.

There were ancient wooden benches along the walls, old golden candle holders with wax that had been melted down eons before, and there was even a green carpet on the floor, large and swirling with gold leaves and magickally preserved from having decayed.

Stairs rose over the foyer in an arch, leading to a second landing. They rippled against the wall either side like twin waterfalls. Ethne stared at the stairs and remarked that they probably led to the temple dormitory and that they should go there to care for Ava's injury and allow her to rest.

They filed deeper inside the foyer, and Liadan, using her magick, closed the great doors behind with her mind, sealing them inside. The room became darker once the doors were closed, and so Ethne took a torch down from the wall, and Liadan lit it with magick for her.

While Ava thought the ancient temple was beautiful, it was also quite spooky and made the hairs rise on her neck. The place was so empty and still and silent . . . and *dark*. Could she really give birth in this dead place? Could she really raise a child here? There were shadows everywhere and all the windows were covered. She wanted to go about dramatically ripping open all the curtains. When they had entered the dormitory and Liadan had laid her down on a narrow bed, Ava begged for someone to open a window.

"We shall, sweet princess," said Lysa, sitting on the edge of the bed and pushing back Ava's sleeve to inspect her injured arm. "Just lie still and try not to exert yourself! Ethne, take that dragon egg before she drops it! Liadan, open the curtains as our princess bids! And one of you light some candles. I can't see my own hand!"

Ava was amused by how automatically Ethne and Liadan obeyed little Lysa. Ethne gently took the dragon egg from Ava and set it on the nightstand in the nest of its soft sling, then set about lighting the candles on the nightstands from her torch, until the room was glowing with light. Meanwhile, Liadan went around the dormitory opening all the curtains, then she went to the hearth on the opposite side of the room and lit the ancient logs there with magick.

"We shall need more firewood before long," said Ethne, warming her hands over the blaze. She sounded tired, as if she were reciting all the chores she dreaded carrying out. "Unless these are *magick* logs that burn for all eternity," she muttered, "and somehow, I doubt they are."

Darkness was falling outside, but with the windows open, the room wasn't as musty and gloomy. The last streams of sunlight reached in, angling across the rows of beds and their white sheets, and fresh air blew through the room, cold and crisp but welcome after the must of the shut-away temple.

Lysa took bandages from her knapsack – which she had managed to hold onto in the chaos—and bound Ava's arm so that she could not move it. She tisked as she told Ava her arm was likely broken but she assured the princess that she would care for her until it was healed.

"Take this for the pain," Lysa said, pressing a leaf on Ava's tongue.

Ava swallowed the bitter leaf and made a face. "Blah! What is it?"

"It will take the pain away," said Lysa. "I picked it out in the forest. Ethne recognized it, and I knew you would need some with this child on the way."

"You're so sweet to me, Lysa," Ava said, gazing up at Lysa happily and so grateful to have her for a friend.

Lysa blushed a little. "Of course, I am, princess. Now hush and lie still. You keep moving your arm, you shall hurt yourself!"

As Lysa was fussing over Ava, Liadan drifted wretchedly from the room. Ava gazed after her sadly, wanting to comfort her.

"I shall go after her," said Ethne at once. "Do not exert yourself, Ava. Just lie there and let Lysa take care of you. If we do not return immediately, it is because we have gone hunting. Our saddlebags with the rations were lost in this madness, and we shall have no food otherwise. The two of you shall be quite safe here." So saying, Ethne turned and marched from the room.

When Ethne had gone, Ava frowned sadly at Lysa. She reached up with her good arm and gently pushed Lysa's hair behind her ear. "You should rest as well, Lysa. It has been a long day."

"It has been a long *life*," Lysa said, making Ava laugh softly, "but I am fine sitting here beside you. I am anxious that all the excitement shall make the baby come soon. I should stay near at hand."

"I am anxious that we have been followed," returned Ava darkly. "We shall stay here until the baby is born. Then I think, when she is a little older, we shall venture deeper into the forest and find another temple, one more hidden away."

"Stop fretting," said Lysa. "That is my job. For right now, rest and content yourself that we are safe. If Ethne is right about the ancient spells over this place, then none may harm us here."

Ava glanced around the room, which had darkened with the setting sun and was glowing gently with candlelight. The fire on the hearth had filled the chilly room with a delicious warmth, and the cold breeze that swept through the window was pleasant by contrast. Gazing around, Ava observed that the beds were neatly made, though some had been left wrinkled and unmade, and there were books open on a low table near the fire, alongside a chair, as if someone had sat there reading. There was also a golden goblet that was, amazingly enough, still full of wine.

"It looks as if the elves just up and left Elloris in the middle of their knitting," Ava said, still gazing around. "It's as if they just left everything and walked out, and the magick of the place preserved the moment."

"You think the chamber pots are still full?" Lysa teased. "Shall I get to cleaning?"

Ava giggled. Lysa laughed as well. Then the gravity of the situation settled over them again, and their laughter weakened to silence in their throats.

Without warning, Lysa leaned down and kissed Ava slowly on the lips. A thrill of pleasure made Ava's heart skip a happy beat. She still felt guilty that Lysa was in love with her, that she kept kissing Ava behind Ethne's back, but Lysa was such a good kisser that Ava didn't have the heart to make her stop.

"I was terrified I would lose you," Lysa said, bowing her head and clutching Ava's small hand in her own. "That you would die with Rowan and Saoirse! But we made it here in one piece, you're alive! The gods were merciful this day!"

"Lysa . . ."

"I'm sorry for kissing you. I have loved you since we were children. I don't suppose I shall ever stop."

"Good," Ava whispered, startling Lysa. "I like it when you kiss me."

Lysa smiled sadly.

"How long do you think Liadan and Ethne shall be away?" Ava said meaningfully. "It has never been just the pair of us, and I could use your sweet comfort about now."

Lysa sat frozen, her eyes bright with happiness, her cheeks flaming. She looked as if she had been offered a fortune in gold. Ava laughed girlishly. Embarrassed, Lysa pushed her hair behind her ear and squeezed Ava's hand. "I would like that greatly, my princess," she whispered happily.

They kissed again, and as their lips caressed, Ava felt Lysa's hand fumble under her skirt and touch her gently throbbing clitoris.

Chapter 3

Liadan wasn't hard to find. The temple was so empty that the slightest movement echoed up and down the halls. Ethne could hear Liadan's heavy footsteps, the jingle of her armor as she walked, and before long, they were walking side by side down a dark corridor, as Ethne held her torch aloft in one hand.

They were silent during their strange stroll. Ethne, having known Liadan for years, understood the ways of the Wildoras and that Liadan, in her grief, needed silence and distraction. If they were to speak, it should be about anything except what had just happened. That was the only way to comfort Liadan.

"This place is truly endless," Liadan said after a while. "Just how long have we been walking?"

"A few days?" Ethne joked.

Liadan managed a small smile.

But the corridor did indeed seem endless. They had been following its twists and turns for several minutes. They passed many dormitories and sitting rooms, chapels, small studies, and solars, and as they did so, it occurred to Ethne how truly large the place was. The amount of priestesses who had once lived here was massive.

Before long, they came to a door at the end of the corridor. It was unlike the other doors, for it was quite large and stood at the bottom of a flight of stairs that were made of gray stone, not the white smooth stone the rest of the building was shaped from. Torches were in brackets on the walls either side this new, mysterious door, and . . . *they were lit.*

Their flames were still standing, still crackling after a thousand years of abandonment.

"This is not normal," Ethne muttered. She looked at Liadan. "Shall we turn back?"

To Ethne's surprise, Liadan was staring at the door like one entranced. She slowly descended the stair, and Ethne followed, a feeling of foreboding in her chest.

When they had reached the bottom of the stair, Ethne was expecting that the door would be difficult to open, perhaps locked or requiring magick, but Liadan grabbed the handle and opened it easily.

"Hmm," said Ethne thoughtfully. She brightened eagerly. "Perhaps it's a wine cellar!"

Liadan didn't answer, instead descending the stair in the same trance. Ethne followed.

They walked down and down through the darkness. The stair carried them around in a spiral, and here, the stone walls were gray as well and pressing close. As they descended, they passed many torches in brackets, also lit with dancing flames. Ethne was beginning to wonder if maybe someone had recently been to the temple and had left the torches lit. The notion did not comfort her: only a person with magick could have opened the temple doors.

They reached the bottom of the stairs at last to find themselves standing in the doorway of an immense and ancient library. Endless row after row of towering wooden bookshelves greeted them, and more books were stacked on the floors, on tables, on the seats of wooden and delicately carved chairs. There were many places with chairs grouped around tables and books open upon the tables, as if only just the hour before, elves had sat there studying. Some of the candles were even still lit.

"The books were preserved with magick, and so was the smell of old parchment, apparently," Ethne complained, making a face. When there was no answer, she glanced over at Liadan. The Knight of the Wild was standing and staring in a sort of trance.

"Liadan! What the hell's the matter with you?" Ethne demanded.

Liadan blinked and looked around, as if shaken from a daydream. "What? Can't you see her? We followed her down the stair!"

Ethne frowned. "See who? Liadan, I think maybe we should head back upstairs so you can rest. I can go hunting alone—"

"Look!" said Liadan, who was gazing at a stack of books not twenty feet away. "She wants us to read that book!" So saying, Liadan marched to the book stack and snatched a book from somewhere in the middle of the pile, causing the others to tumble over.

"Liadan, what—?" Ethne tripped over a book as she followed. She came to Liadan's side and held the torch over her, giving her light to read.

Liadan opened the book and turned through it. She kept pausing and looking in the same direction, as if she were taking directions from someone. It was so bizarre that Ethne was on the verge of insisting they leave when the Knight of the Wild spoke again.

"Here," said Liadan, stopping on a page with curly script and side-panel drawings of towers and dragons. "She wants me to read this page!"

Holding the torch aloft, Ethne leaned over to look at the book and cursed: the writing was, naturally, in a language she couldn't decipher. While knights did learn some elven at the academy, only those knights who planned on becoming explorers bothered with it. The elves had been gone one thousand years and because most of their ruins were confined to Elloris, there was no point in learning their languages.

Liadan, however, seemed perfectly capable of reading the book, and Ethne wasn't surprised: learning the elven languages was a part of Wildoras culture. Some suspected it was because the Wildoras women were related to the elves, for aside from the elves, they alone had magick.

"It speaks of the Godga," said Liadan after a pause.

Ethne frowned. "What!"

Liadan nodded. "It speaks of her," she confirmed. "It says that she is a terrible demon, a dragon trapped in human form, and that she, in her wickedness, once brought fire and bloodshed to the whole of Isliine. She had a cult of worshipers – Wildoras women—and many children were . . . sacrificed in her name."

Ethne went still. "What!" was all she could manage a second time.

"It also says that the only way to hold the Godga is to keep the four watchtowers in-tact . . . The watchtowers were built by some elf named . . . Minye?" Liadan stumbled over the pronunciation. She went on, her eyes scanning the book, "Each watchtower is guarded by one of four dragons, who are sworn to keep the Godga trapped in her human form." Liadan gazed off. "Shite."

"Holy hell," said Ethne. "That lying old hag! She was going to trick us into destroying the watchtowers so that she could, what? Take over the damned world?"

"Sounds like it," said Liadan heavily.

"And now you've made a pact with her. Ava will never give up that dragon egg knowing this! What shall we do?" Ethne wondered.

Liadan gazed off again, as if seeing something Ethne could not.

"And what the devil are you seeing?" Ethne demanded, frustrated. She looked where Liadan was looking and saw only stacks of old books and melted candle wax.

"There's an elven woman," said Liadan. "She haunts this place. She would not see the return of the Godga to power. Apparently," she looked at the book in her hands again, "the Godga is the reason my people were cursed and cast down. My people worshipped her, aided her when she tried to take over the world, but Azmon, he stripped the Godga of her power and exiled her to the edge of the seven realms, where he doomed her with the eternal task of guarding the river."

"And your people were exiled with her," said Ethne. "That doesn't seem fair. I mean, certainly not all of them were cultists!"

"Well," said Liadan darkly, "Azmon may have done a good thing in stopping the Godga, but he also hated women. Ava is right to return us to power, but not with that foul woman's help." She snapped the book shut. "Come. Let us return to Ava and Lysa. I shall go hunting in the morning. This night has gone on long enough."

"True enough," agreed Ethne.

They turned and started back up the stairs, side by side. Liadan was still carrying the book under her arm, and now she looked tired and grim.

"You know," said Ethne after a while, "for a second there I . . . I almost hoped you had seen the spirit of Saoirse or Rowan."

Liadan smiled sadly. "It would have been a great comfort to know they are not angry with me, that they do not blame me for their untimely deaths—"

"What!"

They halted on the stair, and Ethne faced Liadan, still holding the torch aloft.

"Their deaths were not your fault, Liadan!" Ethne said hotly. "They chose to travel with us to Elloris because they loved you and wanted to help you! The fault lies with your blasted sister, who did betray us."

They started up the stairs again, and Ethne thought Liadan looked a little less miserable.

"And you tried to warn me," Liadan said apologetically. "But I did not heed."

"And why should you have? Ceana was your sister. You loved her and trusted her, and she betrayed that trust. Torment yourself not with thoughts of blame. There was nothing you could have done. What matters now is that we are here," Ethne clapped a hand on Liadan's shoulder, "and you are to be a parent! How does that make you feel?"

"Small," said Liadan weakly.

"Hmm. Really?"

"Aye. I want to be a good parent, I want to protect and provide, but I do not want to put so much pressure on my young child. Ava fully intends to retake Caradin, and she likely intends for the child and the dragon to play a large part in it."

"Is that what you want?" Ethne asked quietly. Privately, she didn't believe Liadan wanted any of it.

"I want Ava to be happy," Liadan replied. "If removing men from power shall make her happy, I will cut off every king's head myself."

Liadan sounded so determined that Ethne did not doubt her. "And what is Ava's plan?" she asked.

Liadan sighed. "She believes we should charm Almara to our side."

"Then she's mad," said Ethne at once. "Why the hell would King Elric—?"

"She doesn't wish to appeal to Elric but to Treasa, the queen, which may have been feasible if not for Rowan's death." Liadan swallowed hard, staring at her boots as they walked the dark corridor.

"Rowan's death was not your fault but Eyvor's," said Ethne soothingly. "If anything, Treasa may wish to avenge her daughter. She loved Rowan greatly, and from what I have heard, did give her up most grudgingly, though it was kept from Rowan."

Liadan lifted her brows in surprise. "But why keep that from Rowan?"

"According to my noble mother, to prevent a coup from the women – such as you and Ava intend now," said Ethne, smiling.

"Then perhaps there is hope that Treasa will aid us," said Liadan thoughtfully. "There are many who are loyal to her and who would follow her to our side."

"The queens of the other realms admire Treasa greatly, tis true," Ethne agreed.

Liadan gazed down the torch-lit corridor, into the distance, lost for a moment in thought. "If only we could keep our daughter out of it. I couldn't bear to send my child into battle."

"It may be hard to accept," said Ethne, "but from what the old hag said, your child and that dragon sound as if they shall be mighty and great assets to your cause. The Godga was a lying old snake, but I do believe she was honest about that."

"And you tried to warn us about her as well," apologized Liadan, "and we ignored you. I am sorry we did not take your suspicions seriously."

"You shall learn to start heeding my intuition before long, muttonheads that you all are," Ethne teased.

Liadan smiled briefly, but they both became somber again and walked in silence for a time, and Ethne knew they were both thinking of Saoirse and Rowan, whose lives could have been spared if Ceana had not preyed upon her sister's trust.

They returned to the dormitory to find Ava and Lysa asleep, curled in a narrow bed together, their clothing undone. Ethne thought they looked exquisite. One of Ava's great breasts was hanging out of her gown-front, and the plump mound was rigid with a small, pink nipple. Lysa, meanwhile, was lying with her tunic undone and falling over one naked shoulder, her leather armor forgotten on the floor, her brown hair a mess in her eyes. Ethne thought she looked like an angel as she slept, with her pink cheeks and sweet lips.

The fire was still roaring, and the candles still lit, giving the room of beds a cozy feel that was most welcoming after their long and weary day.

"Shall we separate them?" said Ethne as she and Liadan stood over the bed where Ava and Lysa held each other, sleeping peacefully. "I wanted to sleep with Lysa in my arms tonight, but it seems cruel to part them."

"Let them comfort each other," said Liadan. "I do not deserve sweet Ava in my arms after leading her so blindly into danger." So saying, she went to one of the cushioned armchairs at the fire and flopped down in exhaustion, armor jingling heavily.

Ethne set her torch in a bracket on the wall and followed Liadan, sitting in an armchair opposite. She felt too wearied by the day's events to bother unbuckling her armor and knew Liadan felt the same. And so, they both sat there, slouching and tired, letting the warmth of the fire wash deliciously over them, and thinking of their departed friends.

"Ethne," Liadan said after a while.

Ethne was staring at the fire and answered, "Yes, Li?"

"Do you think there's a place we go to when we die? Do you think Saoirse and Rowan are there? Or is this the only life we get and then nothing. Just darkness."

"I think," said Ethne heavily, "I need a drink."

Liadan laughed sadly.

"Liadan?"

"Yes, Ethne?"

"Whatever happens, I shall be there at your side. Dead or living, darkness or light."

"Oh, joy," Liadan said sarcastically, but they both laughed, and when their laughter had quieted, they smiled at each other and knew it to be true: they would always be together, and they would always be friends.

Chapter 4

When Liadan imparted her grim news in the morning, Lysa had assumed that learning about the Godga's true intentions would upset Ava, but on the contrary, Ava was ecstatic to find information that could give her leverage in her campaign for the throne. The princess could not read ancient elven script herself, of course, so she bid Liadan to guide her to the library, and there, they poured over the books together.

Lysa was further surprised when Ava -—the lazy princess who had never cared for her studies—expressed a desire to learn to read the books herself. Liadan obliged, and Ava was such a quick study, Lysa began to wonder if the legends weren't true and if House Damaris was, in fact, a bloodline of humans who were descendants of the ancient elves.

Liadan and Ava eventually spent so much time alone together in the ancient library that Lysa began to feel jealous. The former handmaiden was very used to having Ava to herself, as it had been that way for years, but now, Ava – in her feverish desire to learn everything she could about successful coups and conquests of old – was spending every waking moment with Liadan. And what was worse, they were engaging in an activity Lysa could not take part in: they were *reading*.

While Ava and Liadan were studying in the ancient library, Lysa and Ethne sat in the barren yard of the ancient temple on broken white bricks, sleeves rolled up, skinning the hares they had captured while hunting that morning. Lysa was very proud of herself. She was proving a decent hunter and had even learned to make sturdy traps for small game. She wanted to be useful to Ava and swelled with pride whenever she returned with a good kill and Ava sang her praises.

It was a beautiful spring morning. New flowers were blooming, and birds were singing. The temple's fragmented yard was lined with cracked stone pathways and pillars. Many of the pathways were fractured and the white pillars had fallen, for the roots of great trees had thrust themselves up from the earth, toppling them over and breaking the laid stone. The ancient forest, so vibrantly green, pressed around the city and pushed its way up between buildings, mighty roots and branches bursting through walls and floors. If the city was falling apart, Lysa knew it was because of the forest. The preservation spell had frozen the city in place, halting all wear and decay, but apparently, it could not stop other influences of destruction.

The city was so wild and overrun by the forest, Lysa and Ethne didn't even have to venture far from the temple to hunt. It wasn't uncommon for unwitting herds of deer to go drifting by the temple beneath the trees, or little rabbits and pheasants to wander too near the temple step. The city ruins were all but one with the forest now, their buildings swallowed by flowers and vines.

Lysa often wondered what would happen if blood were shed on the temple grounds. Ethne had explained that it was hallowed ground, protected by ancient elven magick, but Lysa wasn't entirely certain she understood what that meant. She didn't know much about magick.

As they skinned the hares, their hands bloody, Lysa glanced over at Ethne and thought the Knight of the Sparrow so frustratingly beautiful. Ethne was not wearing her armor, for she seldom hunted in it. Instead, she was wearing a tunic, trousers, and boots, and on her back was a bow and a quiver of arrows with golden feathers. She had taken both from an elven armory there in the city ruins. (Lysa, having explored the armory with Ethne, had taken her own set and was likewise wearing a bow and quiver on her back.)

Ethne's dark hair was in a loose, messy ponytail, the tie of which was nearly at the tip of her tresses, and she was sitting with her knees spread as she worked, her sleeves rolled back to reveal her bulging arms.

"If it makes you feel any better, I doubt they are actually *reading* down there," Ethne joked, trying to comfort Lysa when she noticed her pouting over her work.

"It doesn't make me feel better," Lysa grumbled—then, catching herself, "I mean, I'm n-not bothered! Ava and Liadan are married now. Why shouldn't they spend time together?"

Ethne laughed, not convinced. "You love Ava and do wish you held sway over her heart as Liadan does. It's all right, fair Lysa." She added bitterly, "I can sympathize."

Lysa glanced at Ethne apologetically, then they continued skinning in silence. They had been at the temple three days already, but Lysa and Ethne hadn't lain together once.

Lysa had, in fact, been bedding Ava as much as she could whenever Liadan and Ethne were away. She knew the other two were aware of it, and while Liadan seemed indifferent – and preoccupied with grieving her friends, as well as thoughts of parenthood – Ethne was not indifferent at all. The Knight of the Sparrow tried to appear as if she didn't care, but Lysa could see her growing bitterness.

Little more than a week before, Ethne had killed Rois—an old lover who she had cared for greatly—in Lysa's defense. And Lysa was repaying her by lying with Ava when her back was turned? Lysa felt low. She felt like scum. She felt like the dog she was always accusing Ethne of being, even though it was more than just sex, even though she loved and adored Ava.

"Perhaps tonight we could share a bed in the dormitory," Lysa said casually, hoping to appease Ethne.

Ethne kept her eyes on her work, and her expression was cold. "Wouldn't you rather care for Ava? She is still doing poorly with that broken arm. No doubt she would miss your . . . comfort."

"Yes, if only *Fionn* were here to mend her arm, perhaps she wouldn't need my comfort," Lysa shot back.

Ethne halted, glaring at Lysa. "You persist in dragging me through the mud for having lain with Fionn, while you were off getting spit-roasted by Saoirse and Rowan—!"

Lysa blushed to her hairline.

"Yes, I saw you!" Ethne said scathingly. "One between your thighs and the other at your mouth. Perhaps if I'd had as many hands as Eyslath, you wouldn't have strayed—"

"Perhaps if I understood how much I meant to you," Lysa said over her.

"How much you meant? I asked you to marry me!"

"Only because Liadan asked Ava! And then *directly* after, you bedded that slave girl on the *Golden Rose* – *Yes*, I know! I saw the way she kissed you farewell!—and you *also* fucked Rois—!"

Ethne winced.

"—and *then* you bedded *every* tavern wench in Hadun—!"

"Don't be dramatic," said Ethne wearily. "It was more like two of them, and one I only kissed, for the love of—"

"And you still won't talk about Rois!"

The name left Ethne stricken. She swallowed hard, dropped her eyes to her work, and kept skinning.

Lysa didn't understand why Ethne wouldn't let her in, wouldn't share the most intimate parts of her. She spoke often of wanting to be close, of wanting to be in love, yet did not allow for true intimacy to happen between them.

Back when they were traveling the snow-swept roads in southern Illa, Ethne had spoken of Rois, but very briefly and in passing, as if it were just too painful a wound to prod. Lysa had respected that boundary, for at the time, they had barely known each other. There was no reason to pry.

But now it had been weeks, and they had lain together many times, they had shared meals, they had shared beds. Could they not share what was in their hearts as well? Lysa found it amazing that Ethne found it so easy to bury her face between her thighs yet could not talk to her about a woman from her past.

Having finished skinning her hare, Lysa stood, the bald, pink hare dangling in her fist, and said, "When you are ready to talk to me about Rois, I shall be waiting." With that, she dropped the hare in her bucket with the others and carried the pale inside, leaving Ethne alone in the ruined yard.

THAT EVENING, AS AVA and Lysa prepared for bed in the dormitory, Liadan and Ethne stood on the roof of one of the temple's great towers, and there, Liadan practiced casting magick at a straw dummy Ethne had brought her from the nearby armory.

Liadan was convinced that either Eyvor's men or orcs or perhaps even more temple knights from Hastow would be upon them soon and had insisted on practicing her casting and swordplay every evening since their arrival at the temple. She and Ethne had ventured to the armory for this reason and had been careful to carry back everything they could to the temple of Erinyel, so worried were they that their enemies might find some way inside the armory and clean it of weapons and arms now that Liadan had broken the ancient seal locking the place away.

Ethne sometimes practiced sparring with Liadan, but that evening, she stood with her hands behind her back, watching as Liadan cast golden fireballs at a straw dummy – which was black and charred but hadn't completely incinerated because Liadan was holding back. If the Knight of the Wild were to cast full force, the dummy would vanish into a pile of ash, Ethne knew.

Neither of the knights were in their armor and were instead wearing tunics and trousers. Liadan's sleeves were rolled up, revealing the bulge of her strong arms as she waved her hands, practicing the gesture before casting.

"What troubles you?" Liadan said, though her frowning eyes were fixed on the dummy. She cast again, and the golden light of her magick briefly illuminated her face as it floomed into the strawman.

"Lysa. What else?" said Ethne with a toneless laugh.

"What is the quarrel now?" prompted Liadan, and she cast another fireball at the strawman, which trembled as it was hit. "If I didn't know any better, I would think you two were already married, the way you carry on."

Ethne sighed. "Lysa wants me to talk about my past. She wants me to talk about Rois."

"She wants intimacy," said Liadan, nodding as she stared down the strawman. She cast another fireball, and the strawman rustled as it rocked in place.

"Yes," said Ethne heavily. "And I don't know how to give it to her. I don't know how to be that. . . . vulnerable. All the women I've been with have just wanted sex. They asked for nothing more, and I was content with that. Hell, I was ecstatic."

Liadan laughed. "Except now you aren't," she reminded Ethne. "You wanted a relationship with Lysa. You wanted marriage. It requires vulnerability, Ethne. It means sharing who you are. How else shall she love thee if she can't even know thee? You cannot close your heart to her and expect love in return."

Ethne sighed again. "True enough. I suppose I should be more . . . *open*." She winced out the last word, as if she had tasted something foul as she spoke it, and Liadan laughed at her wincing.

"What the devil have you and Lysa been talking about all this time if you have not been open?" Liadan asked in amazement. She cast another fireball. *Floom.* "I have seen you exchanging whispers on the road, and when we stayed at an inn, you sometimes took a corner seat at the tavern and spoke then as well."

Ethne shrugged. "In the beginning I just whispered sweet nothings to make her toes curl."

Liadan laughed. "Of course, you did," she said, shaking her head in amusement. She cast another fireball. *Floom. Rustle. Hiss.*

"Then sometimes we would talk of our shared loves, the things we liked to do and see. Lysa loves the sea, and I did confess once that I liked knitting. She had a good laugh about that."

Liadan smiled, casting another fireball. *Floom.* "So you were off to a good start, then. At least."

Ethne shrugged again. "The little things are easy to talk about. It's the big things that are hard. Rois was a big thing, and Lysa insists on digging into it."

"I think she hath won the right, don't you?" said Liadan. *Floom. Rustle. Hiss.* "She was beside herself when you did flee in Adwean. And then she and I nearly died trying to rescue you from Rois, who you ran to willingly. Rois would have killed her had you not stepped in, and you took your time stepping in, did you not?"

"I *cared* about Rois!" Ethne protested. "She was the first woman I ever truly cared for! I mean, I never loved her, there was no time for that, but I believe I could have! If her father hadn't been such a bastard, she and I would have been so happy together. She needn't have become a slaver! Living and breathing with this wound, why should I have rushed to end Rois' life? In the end, she couldn't help what she became."

"Lysa should hear all of this, not I, for I doth know it already," answered Liadan, a little breathless now from her exertions. She stopped and dragged her wrist across her brow, gazing at Ethne. After a moment, her eyes moved past Ethne and she laughed hoarsely. "And now I suppose our Lysa does as well."

Ethne turned and halted: Lysa was standing at the hatch door which led to the tower below. She was looking directly at Ethne and her brown eyes were sympathetic.

"I shall go down and start supper," Liadan said, clapping Ethne on the shoulder as she passed. She glanced once over Lysa and smacked her on the backside as she moved past her, making her blush and squeal.

When Liadan had gone, Lysa drew near to Ethne, gazing up at her. "I had no idea you were going through all of that!" she cried. "Why not share it with me?"

Ethne shrugged miserably. "I didn't think you'd care to share it. Perhaps because you were too busy getting finger-fucked by my friends."

Lysa blushed. "Well, I'm here now, aren't I? It would have been you who touched me in Hastow if I weren't so angry about the . . . Well, every woman you laid with between Wedale and Hargendon."

Ethne started to turn away, but Lysa grabbed her hands, pulling her back around. As they faced each other, Lysa peered imploringly into Ethne's face.

"It's time to let go of the past, I think," said the former handmaiden. "Saoirse and Rowan are gone. The pain of it haunts me night and day, but I know tis nothing compared to what you endure. If you need me, I am here, though I know Liadan were probably the better listening ear."

Ethne smiled gratefully. "My thanks," without warning, she took Lysa in her arms and kissed her gently on the lips, "sweet Lysa."

Caught in Ethne's hard embrace, Lysa's lashes fluttered in pleasant surprise. She gazed breathlessly up at Ethne, and Ethne was reminded for one moment of the flustered and seemingly sweet little handmaiden she had been back in southern Illa, back before she learned to fight and ride, when she had depended on Ethne so readily and had doted on her skill with a blade. Ethne missed those days when Lysa had needed her. It had only been a few weeks, but it seemed so long ago now.

Now Ethne was the one who needed Lysa. She used to think she would hate feeling this vulnerable, feeling this dependent, but . . . she enjoyed it. She found herself trembling.

"What's the matter?" whispered Lysa, whose voice had become hushed and intimate after their kiss. Her concerned eyes danced up and down Ethne's trembling arms, which bulged with muscles around her, and she smoothed her little hand over Ethne's cheek, as if to calm her.

"Can't you see how desperately I need you?" Ethne whispered back. "If you were to die like Rowan and S-Saoirse—" Ethne choked to silence when sudden tears rose to blind her.

Lysa frowned in sympathy, her little thumb smoothing over Ethne's bottom lip to catch a tear. "Hush, my knight," she whispered and kissed Ethne on the lips. "I shall not leave you. Not for a long time to come." She smiled mischievously.

Ethne laughed through her tears, and they kissed.

Chapter 5

Since coming to the temple of Erinyel, Liadan and Ethne had spent a great deal of time together, sparring on the rooftops of the temple's great towers, hunting for long hours straight into the evening, sometimes just sitting beside the fire in one of the solars and drinking and brooding in silence together. Ava watched the women with Lysa from afar, and both were concerned, for so distraught were the knights that they never once made a move to lay with either of them.

Ava knew Liadan and Ethne were mourning their friends. The loss of Saoirse and Rowan had been so brutal and sudden. They had passed through the city gate, and just like that, both women were gone. One moment their group was all laughter and joy, the next they were fighting for their lives against King Eyvor's men. And now Liadan was without guidance, without her mentor, without two of her sisters in arms – without her actual sister, who had betrayed her—and Ethne was just as lost. They were like two baffled children, uncertain and sad, wandering the halls of Erinyel as if they would find their friends somewhere inside. Ava knew that both knights blamed themselves: Liadan for not listening to Ethne and Ethne for not protesting louder.

But in truth, Ava knew that the fault lay with her father, King Eyvor, who had apparently sent men to kill her and her unborn! She still couldn't believe it! She remembered how the men had yelled for Ceana to kill Ava, to not let her get away, and couldn't connect those grim men and their orders to the kind-eyed blonde man who had raised her. But, kind as King Eyvor had *sometimes* been, he had always been a ruthless and pragmatic king. And he had a bastard son now to sit on the throne. If he thought Ava was pregnant, then she was a threat to him and his son, a threat to be eliminated.

Ava was tempted to be sad and angry and perhaps wallow in the misery for a few days, but she knew it was time for her finally grow up, that she had a child on the way whose future was at stake as much as her own. She needed to accept her circumstances for what they were, and she needed to fight back until Caradin and all of Isliine were hers. And so, Ava toiled in the ancient library the night through, Liadan ever at her side, interpreting the elven script Ava struggled to understand, knowing that one day she would ride against her father *and* Bjorn and take back what was hers!

And Ava thought it was a marvelous stroke of luck – or perhaps a blessing of the gods – that she should find her way to the temple of Erinyel, the elven goddess of secrets. The library beneath the temple was, as a result, a treasure trove of knowledge. There were many hidden things here, things most of the world was never meant to know, things that had been hidden away for centuries.

There were several books on the Godga, for instance, all of them detailing the old woman's many centuries of life. Apparently, the Godga had been born a dragon but had sought human form so that she could walk among humans. When she was slain in dragon form, her spirit passed into the body of a woman – a human queen—and apparently, she had been hopping from body to body for centuries, it being the method with which she preserved her immortality.

Reading about the Godga filled Ava with foreboding, for she was beginning to understand exactly why the Godga wanted one of her children. If Ava handed over the dragon, then the Godga could possess it and become a dragon once more, and if Ava handed over her daughter . . . Then the Godga could possess her and become a young and beautiful sorceress again. The idea of the old woman doing either was horrifying.

They had been at Erinyel's ancient temple for one week when Ava, quite large with child, knelt with difficulty beside the roaring hearth in the dormitory and – as she had every night since coming to the temple – placed her dragon egg in the flames. She used a poker to turn the egg, slowly letting it warm on each side, and sometimes when the fire was bright enough, she could see the dragonling's silhouette curled inside.

That night, as Ava performed her nightly ritual with the egg, she saw the silhouette yet again. This time it moved, wiggling wildly, and Ava's heart leapt with excitement.

"I think it's hatching!" Ava cried, her eyes large with joy. Behind her, Liadan and Ethne were talking at the window, while Lysa sat on one of the beds, brushing her hair. Now all of them drew near, staring with the same excitement at the egg in the flames.

And indeed, there was a loud crack, and Ava saw a piece of the solid green shell chip and flake away, revealing the side of a scaly hide. Another crack, and there was a chirp like a bird, and Ava could see a little nose – two green nostrils that snorted smoke.

"By the gods!" Ethne gasped when the baby dragon's head had suddenly burst from the egg.

The little head had two gold horns protruding from the temples, and pearly white, sharp teeth. Impatient now, the dragonling wiggled and kicked, sending green fragments of its egg flying. It slowly pushed free, slithering from the egg almost like a snake. Its body was long and thin, and two leathery, batlike wings were upon its back, and its tiny eyes were bright gold, the reptilian slits narrowed against the firelight.

"It's beautiful!" Ava breathed as the dragon, spying her, climbed up into her lap and curled against her large belly like a cat, as if it had recognized her. Ava wasn't surprised: she had spent weeks cradling the egg, singing to it, whispering to it. Perhaps the dragon knew her scent.

"I can't believe it," said Lysa, sinking to her knees beside Ava. She stared, spellbound, at the dragonling, which chirped happily against Ava. "That thing was a thousand years old, and it still hatched!"

"Hmm," said Liadan. She and Ethne were standing over Ava and Lysa, and the knights were out of their armor, wearing instead their tunics and trousers. Liadan's bulging arms were folded as she observed the baby dragon curled happily in Ava's embrace. "I wonder what we shall feed a baby dragon," she said thoughtfully.

"Lots of meat. Whole pheasants, rabbits, whatever small game we can find," said Ava with confidence, and when everyone looked at her, she recoiled shyly and added with a blush, "I read it in a story once."

"Princess," said Lysa wearily, "stories aren't true! But I'll admit, feeding a young dragon lots of meat makes sense. I mean, it's a dragon. They aren't vegetarians." So saying, she hesitated and stroked the dragonling's scaly neck with one gentle finger. The dragonling shivered under her caress and chirped happily.

Ethne was the only one not speaking. She stood with her hands in her pockets, looking very grim. The others were happy, excited, intrigued. Ethne, as ever, looked skeptical. She stared at the dragonling in dark contemplation.

Ava sighed. "What, Ethne?" she asked with apprehension. "You have an unfortunate knack for observing terrible, terrible things. So what is it this time?"

"I take no pleasure in observing it, princess," Ethne returned heavily, "but remember what the Godga said? The terms of the pact dictated that you would give up your second child if the old witch slayed the Dragon of Almara for you. We thought she meant you would give her the dragon, which was bad enough, but now . . ." Ethne's slanted eyes went to Ava's big belly.

Ava gasped and placed a protective hand over her protruding belly. "No!" she said angrily at once. "She shall not take my daughter! She shall not!" And Ava didn't know why, but she burst into tears. They rose to blind her, and she wept and wept bitterly into her hand, her broken arm curled against her side in its makeshift sling. With her eyes closed, she could feel Lysa rubbing her shoulder, and Liadan's large hand – so gentle and yet so strong – stroked Ava's hair.

"There, there, wife," Liadan said softly. "I shall not allow the Godga to take our child. This I vow."

Ava's sniffles quieted, but she knew that if the Godga wanted their daughter, there was nothing Liadan or anyone could do. What had she done in making promises to that vile old woman? And now her child would be taken from her, one way or another.

"I suspect when the girl is grown," went on Ethne apologetically, "the Godga will come for her." She looked at Liadan. "You know how fast your people's children grow. We don't have much time."

Liadan was still stroking Ava's hair, but now her determined eyes were on Ava's belly. Ava was startled by the tight anger in Liadan's stance. Liadan was always so calm and slow to rage, but now she looked downright furious. And Ava didn't blame her: the pair of them had been tricked! They had agreed to the Godga's terms, believing she would come to take the dragon away, not their child! But the dragon – who Ava did indeed consider a child of hers – had been born first, and their human child would be born second.

"What shall we do?" Ava wondered wretchedly. As if to soothe her, the dragonling climbed up against her chest and nuzzled under her chin. She smiled sadly and hugged it in her arm, her frightened eyes on the fire as she knelt there, lost in thought.

"This is still hallowed ground," said Liadan firmly. "The Godga cannot make trouble here. If the legends are true, then she is a dragon, and even a dragon cannot disturb elven land that is hallowed. We are safe for the time being, at least."

Ava sniffled miserably. She knew if she spoke, she would burst into tears again. When she glanced around, she noticed Lysa and Ethne staring at her in sympathy.

"Come, my wife," Liadan whispered and lovingly gathered Ava into her strong arms, lifting her as if she weighed absolutely nothing, despite her large belly. Liadan kissed Ava on the forehead and said to her, "You should rest." And so saying, she carried Ava away to one of the beds.

Ava let her head fall against Liadan, silently grateful for her Knight of the Wild.

AS THE SPRING GREW warmer, as flowers blossomed in colorful clouds, and as the last dregs of snow melted away, Ava gave birth to a beautiful baby girl with a head full of her curly blonde hair and Liadan's blue, blue eyes. As Ava had wished, they named the girl Riona after her ancestor, and it wasn't long before little Riona was running around the temple on stubby legs, getting into things and upsetting the furniture. She and the baby dragon were wild and never seemed to rest, climbing the walls and the drapes late into the night as the adults tried and failed to sleep.

Luckily, Liadan had managed to salvage her saddlebags after the skirmish outside of Hadun, and so, all her market purchases of fabric and string were preserved. The Knight of the Wild sat up many nights, sewing together trousers and tunics, bonnets and swaddling for a child that was growing too fast to be true.

Sitting in a chair opposite Liadan as she breastfed their tiny daughter beside the fire, Ava would watch Liadan sewing and try not to laugh, but it was so – *odd* – to see such a large woman with such large fingers and bulging arms, sewing dainty little pants and socks. But Liadan was quite good at it, and because Ava couldn't sew a kerchief to save her life, she daren't mock her wife for having a skill so valuable.

Ava was soon to discover that little Riona was as barbaric and demanding as Liadan. Often when she wanted breastmilk, the infant would climb up on Ava's lap, and ignoring whatever it was her mother was doing at the time, she would yank open Ava's gown and just start suckling. Ava, startled and amused, would cradle her small daughter's head and smile lovingly down at her as she fed, saying under breath, "Just like your other mother, aren't you?"

Ava's breasts were so ripe and swollen with milk that they were often fat as melons and the tiny nipples jutting. She could see how her swollen cleavage distracted the others, and she enjoyed how they stared with lust as her fat breast swelled against Riona's hungrily sucking mouth. They wanted her – Liadan, Ethne, and Lysa, all three of them, but Ava refused their nightly advances while relishing in their flirting. Ethne, especially, became very flirtatious, often joking about the things she would like to do to Ava's breasts, while Lysa listened and blushed with arousal.

Liadan hadn't been allowed to suckle Ava's breasts since they first filled with milk (for the milk was for their daughter, Ava declared in much amusement), and her sex was still healing from giving birth. And so, being off-limits as she was, the others were naturally driven mad over what they could not have.

Ava imagined Liadan would corner her as soon as she was ready once more for pleasure. She could see it always in Liadan's blue eyes, how the Knight of the Wild fantasized about tearing Ava's clothes off, groping her, fingering her, and how she suffered to restrain herself. And Ava, preoccupied and tired as she was with raising their daughter, had to admit she missed lying with Liadan just as much. Some nights, as the others slept, she imagined Liadan's strong, hungry hands on her body, and she shivered under the sheets.

And so, the weeks went by, and little Riona continued, overnight, to grow. And amazingly enough, so did the dragon! The third week after Riona's birth, the child was large enough to have been a six-year-old and was running, walking, and talking—and endlessly asking questions—while the dragon, now the size of a dog, was ever at her side, chirping like a bird and swinging its scaly green tail.

Ava often thought Riona was a tiny, blonde version of Liadan. The child had the supernatural strength of a woman of Wildoras and often had to be scolded to put the furniture down. If she threw a tantrum, then it meant chairs and beds were going to break, perhaps stone walls would be burst through, and in those chaotic moments, only Liadan could handle the child without fear, for the little girl did not yet know her strength and was a danger to the others.

Thankfully, however, little Riona was mostly a calm, sweet-tempered girl, and so, her tantrums were few, even during her toddler stage. She was a curious child, and the questions were unending. She wanted to know everything about her world, starting with the temple they were in, and because Ethne had undergone bard training – which entailed knowing a great deal of legends and myths – it was often to Ethne that Riona wound up going with her questions. After a while, it wasn't uncommon for Ava to return from the library to find little Riona on "Aunt Ethne's" lap, her legs dangling, as the Knight of the Sparrow told her the legends of the ancient elves.

Sometimes the group would take their supper in one of the solars, and as the fire roared nearby, Riona would ask questions about her family and why they were there at the temple instead of being with the rest of House Damaris. Ava answered readily about the great history of House Damaris, but when it came time to answer Riona's questions about her house's current state, she didn't know that she could.

That night at supper, Riona wanted to know why they weren't living at Caradin and were instead hiding in an old temple across the sea. Sitting at the small round table, Ava paused over her plate, fork in hand, and caught eyes with Liadan. Liadan looked back at Ava helplessly and didn't seem ready to explain their exile any more than she.

"Tell the girl," said Ethne, frowning. Her cheek bulged with a hunk of bread she had bitten, and she stared across the table at Ava and Liadan. Her slanted gray eyes were almost scolding.

"She's old enough to ask the question," Ethne insisted, "then she's old enough for an answer."

Lysa hesitated and added, "I agree with Ethne."

Ethne snorted. "That's a first," she said, returning to her stew. She smiled when Lysa elbowed her.

Lysa looked between Ava and Liadan again, her eyes imploring as she said, "Before long, Riona will be a woman, and you will need her help in the fight for Isliine. You might as well tell her now."

Ava took a shaky breath and gazed across the table at her daughter. Riona was the size of a ten-year-old now, and already, she was beautiful. She looked a great deal like Ava, with her long blonde hair and Ava's pink lips, but Liadan's blue eyes were always gazing from her face. Her cheeks were painted with the swirls and lines of warpaint, for she had begged Liadan to help her look more like a Wildoras warrior, and that afternoon had been spent playing "huntress" in the kitchens with the dragon, who she had named Wulfa.

"We were exiled from Caradin," said Ava heavily, "because Liadan slew a prince in my defense when he did try to harm me."

Riona gasped, her pretty blue eyes flying wide.

"This after your grandfather the king attempted to separate us," added Liadan, "and force your mother to an arranged marriage. Your mother and I wanted to be together more than anything, so we fled. Now your grandfather has placed a bastard on the throne as his heir in your mother's stead, and we seek to take back the land that is rightfully hers."

To all of this, Riona listened with her mouth hanging open. Then she shrugged and said, "All right then!" They watched as she gulped her small ale and then bounced up and ran out, having finished her meal. The dragon, which had been lurking under the table for scraps, happily ran after her.

"Well," said Ava, looking over at Liadan in surprise, "that was easy."

Chapter 6

With the others in the solar talking about their grim things over breakfast, Riona decided to take the opportunity to explore the old library under the temple. Her mother never let her go down there alone, fearing that she would get lost in the endless avenues of books, for the library was vast – so vast that Liadan and Ava still hadn't discovered every room and section after nearly two months of having been there.

Ethne had attempted to scare Riona away from the library by telling her exaggerated stories of her and Liadan's encounters with ghosts and giant spiders, but Riona had only giggled at her playful aunt and ignored her. She actually liked it when Ethne tried to frighten her, for it was one of the few times the knight seemed genuinely happy and playful.

For the duration of Riona's very brief childhood, the adults had all been sad and gloomy, and Riona didn't understand why. Sometimes they broke their angst to play with her or entertain her, but for the most part, they did not.

Liadan – who Riona understood to be her father – often sat beside the fire in the dormitory, drinking a tankard of ale, her wild red hair tousled. Should little Riona crawl into the big woman's lap, she was always relieved when Liadan's blue eyes would soften, and the knight's big hand would lovingly stroke Riona's hair. Riona would curl against her father and fall asleep, feeling warm and safe in the knight's bulging arms. She knew that was how her mother must've felt anytime Liadan held her.

Riona loved her parents. Ava was beautiful and clever, always pouring over books and debating back and forth about war strategy and politics with the others in the solar. Riona would sit on the floor and play with her wooden toys – toys which Liadan had carved for her – and the adults didn't realize it, but she was always listening. She found all of it fascinating. She thought her mother was very clever and bright, and she often wondered why Auntie Ethne so often called Ava a "featherhead." The insult was given jokingly, and Ava didn't seem to mind, but Riona still found it baffling.

Auntie Lysa wasn't book-smart like Ava, but she was sharp in her own way. She taught Riona many clever and useful things, like how to tie different knots, how to pick various locks, and how to carry a great deal of things in her pockets. She also taught Riona how to properly wield a dagger and hide it away, though Riona thought it was silly and a waste of time. She would much rather learn the sword!

While Riona loved and looked up to Ava for her prettiness and cleverness, while she loved Ethne's stories and loved Lysa's unapologetic nature, she idolized Liadan. Once when she was still small, after she had begged to go hunting with Liadan, she and her father were out in the city ruins, walking among the giant moss-covered trees, when they happened across a party of orcs who were also hunting for game in the area. There were three of them, big and strong barbarian women, with bulging muscles, covered in skins and furs and beads. They were dark green and had tusks protruding from her lips! Their black hair was wild, their black eyes beady, and Riona gazed at them in awe. She had never seen an orc before. One of the orc women had already caught a deer and had it slung over her shoulder.

Liadan had noticed the orc women before Riona and was standing very still, coldly observing them. Riona started forward to greet the strangers and was shocked when her father held out her arm to stop her. Riona halted, gazing up at Liadan in confusion.

And then it happened: without preamble, without a word, the orcs suddenly attacked. Liadan gently shoved Riona back, telling her to run and hide. Riona didn't want to, but she obeyed, running behind a shattered white wall, through which a gigantic tree had forced itself. She peered around the wall and watched in amazement: already, one of the orc women was screaming, having caught a face full of fire when Liadan outstretched her hand. She fell to the ground, thrashing against the flames, and then was still and silent.

The other two orcs had attacked Liadan in unison, attempting to forestall more magick, and it was working: Liadan was forced to stop casting and bring up her shield, blocking the heavy swing of a chipped two-handed axe. Riona watched, terrified, as her father was backed into a tree by the two orcs, who guffawed evilly around their tusks, but Liadan didn't look terrified at all. The Knight of the Wild had a calm, cold expression as she bashed one orc in the face with her shield – breaking its tusks in a splash of blood – and brought her sword around in a pirouette, taking off the other orc's head.

Riona stared, her mouth hanging open, as the orc's shocked head went bouncing along the ground, trailing blood. With two of the orcs down and one remaining, Liadan was quick to close in on the last one and finish her, driving her sword without hesitation through the woman's bare middle. She rippled the blazing blade free, and the orc – coughing blood – fell in a heap to the ground and was still.

Liadan sheathed her blade, turned, and immediately went to Riona's hiding place, calling for her. Her blue eyes were – for the first time – frightened.

"I'm fine, Father!" Riona squealed, scrambling out from behind the wall. She ran to Liadan and looked up at the big woman in awe. "That was amazing! Can you teach me? Can you?" She bounced up and down.

Liadan seemed pleased that Riona was safe and touched her yellow hair with soft-eyed affection. "Perhaps," was all she said as she turned away. Riona watched as her father stooped, carefully gathered the dead deer one of the orcs had dropped, and slung it over her shoulder as if it weighed nothing. They had then walked back to the temple – Riona bouncing beside Liadan and babbling away in amazement all the while – and it was that day that Riona had decided she wanted to be a knight like her father.

Though Liadan had been very stoic and reserved about agreeing to teach Riona, she did as her daughter wished, and in the month that followed, Riona, under her father's tutelage, grew into a young woman and warrior in her own right. One day, when Riona had grown enough to have been the same age as her own young parents, Liadan took her daughter to the elven armory and helped her find a sword and a set of armor that would fit her. Riona chose an ancient silver sword, a silver elven shield with the sigil of a dragon on it ("Fitting," Liadan had said), and a beautifully engraved silver set of armor with a deep blue cape (for it matched her eyes), and when they returned to the temple, she knew the others found her quite impressive.

Present-day Riona, a young woman in her elven knight armor, conjured a wisp-light over her shoulder, and by its glow, she descended the stair into the ancient library. She could read all the books here, for Liadan had taken great care to teach her, and given the fact that she could grow incredibly fast, she could learn incredibly fast as well. Liadan had explained that it was in her blood to take to elven script so easily, for both her parents were descendants of the ancient elves.

Riona stopped at the bottom of the stair when she heard a frightened whimper and looked back. Wulfa was huddled on the stair behind her, hunched up and wide-eyed. The dragon was now about the size of a young bull but somehow still managed to squeeze through the halls of Erinyel's temple to follow Riona about. It had been at Riona's side since she was born, her parents said, and if she was honest, Riona couldn't imagine herself without it.

"Then stay here, wussy scales," Riona teased the dragon.

Wulfa snorted indignantly, and as if to prove her bravery, the dragon lifted her chin and squeezed her way down the stair and into the library.

Side by side, girl and dragon wandered through the ancient bookshelves, the gold wisp-light hovering over them like a little sun, casting long shadows across the floor. It was so still and silent here that every footstep could be heard, and the scratch of Wulfa's heavy claws on the stone floor almost echoed in the silence.

Ethne had told Riona once that dragons used to be able to talk, that they were intelligent and self-aware but over time, had been reduced to wild and mindless beasts. Wulfa didn't seem mindless. Riona hoped that one day she would speak, and the dragon would speak back.

"Why have you come, daughter of light?"

At the sound of the voice, Riona halted and so did Wulfa, the dragon shivering in fear. Riona looked at the dragon in amazement, thinking it ridiculous that a creature who *breathed fire* should be afraid of anything. Then her eyes went past the shivering dragon, and she froze: a beautiful woman was standing beside a low table filled with books. She was elven, tall and pale, with long blonde hair falling to her feet. Her pale hair was pushed back behind her shoulders to reveal her pointed ears, and she was wearing a white gown, loose and nearly translucent, so that Riona could see the shape of her hips and full breasts through the fabric. Riona felt her sex stir for the first time in her life and blushed faintly in shock.

The elven woman, as if she sensed Riona's desire, smiled softly in amusement. "I am Minye," she said in a sweet, pretty voice that was pleasant to Riona's ears, "and this is my ancient library. I was a priestess of Erinyel once, and I channeled many of the books that are here.

The great goddess, in her mercy and wisdom, did bequeath the secret knowledge to me."

"You're . . ." Riona took an absent step forward, "beautiful!"

The elven woman smiled.

Riona heard Wulfa groan, and when she glanced over, the dragon was actually rolling her eyes! Riona was flushed with irritation for a moment, then she realized the dragon could see the woman as well.

"My dragon can see you," Riona said to the elven woman. "Does that mean you're real?"

"I am real," answered the woman patiently. "I am also a spirit."

Riona swallowed hard. "Oh," was all she could manage. Now she suddenly understood why the others had warned her away from the library: they were worried that she would see the spirit who lingered here and that it would frighten her. But Riona wasn't frightened. The elven woman was beautiful, utterly beautiful, but somehow reminded her of her mother. She looked in Minye's green eyes and was reminded of Ava's sweet green eyes looking down at her as she breastfed when a babe.

Minye tilted her head curiously. "You did not answer my question. Why have you come, daughter of light?"

"I come seeking knowledge," Riona answered honestly. "My mother wishes to take back Illa and all the realms for women. I wish to aid her in any way I can."

"Why?" Minye asked abruptly. She folded her pretty hands before her, and her sleeves draped down like wings. Riona thought she suddenly looked cold and regal, as if she were guarding the knowledge of her great library from intruders, as if she might banish Riona if she answered incorrectly.

"Because I want my parents to be happy," Riona answered honestly. "Because I don't want to hide in a temple the rest of my life." She frowned as she added, "Because the world should be ruled by women."

Minye smiled, as if Riona had said something rehearsed and predictable, and Riona blushed more hotly in embarrassment.

"But how do you know this without having experienced the world?" Minye asked gently.

"Because it was men who banished my parents! It was men who tried to have me murdered before I was even born! And it is men who are tearing the seven kingdoms apart with war even now!" Riona answered more hotly than she intended.

While it was true that she hadn't experienced the world or even encountered a man before – and indeed, men might as well have been mythological creatures, for even the orcs she had seen were women – Riona knew enough to understand that it was because of men that she lived in exile, hiding away in a temple in the middle of ancient ruins. She had listened often to her parents speaking of it when she was smaller and they had thought her asleep, she had heard Auntie Ethne weep at night for want of her homeland. She knew what had happened to her family was deeply wrong, and she would do anything to rectify it. She did not want Caradin to be a dream her mother relived to her at the fire every night before bed. She did not want Caradin to be a story.

Riona was on the verge of relating her thoughts to the spirit, but she had the feeling Minye had already heard them. The elven woman was smiling and nodded in approval.

"Your spirit is strong," said Minye, still smiling. "I will tell you how to attain what you seek, but it is a quest you must venture alone." Her slanted green eyes went to the dragon. "Well, your dragon may aid you. But you must leave your parents and their friends behind."

Riona frowned. "But why? I c-can't leave them here! They are all I've ever—!" She bit her lip and quickly fell silent when she realized how childish she sounded.

Minye smiled patiently. "Will you come or no?"

Riona took a shaking breath. "I will do whatever it takes to see the end of the age of man."

Minye smiled.

More From Ash Gray

Her First Knight
Book 8
The Daughter of Light
Chapter 1

Riona knew her parents would try to stop her leaving on her own, that they wouldn't understand the reason she must take the quest with Wulfa, and that they would come after her, frantic to protect her, for though Riona was very much now a woman, her parents still saw her as their little girl. It had, after all, only taken her two months to mature. And so, after writing her family a letter in farewell, the wild young knight with warpaint on both cheeks set out with Wulfa from the temple, leaving the halls of Erinyel and their safety behind.

Riona's letter had been painfully vague, she knew, but if she had told her family where she was going, they would have followed, and it was simply too dangerous, even for Liadan.

While training with her father, Riona had quickly realized that she was more powerful than Liadan, being able to cast fireballs that could bring down an entire village, and Ava—frightened for Riona's safety—would have tried to convince her daughter to take back the seven realms the typical way, by gathering allies and sending forth armies to do their fighting. She would not believe Riona that there was another way, which was ironic, Riona thought: while Ava abhorred male violence and war, she was perfectly willing to engage in it, rather than searching for some other way to attain her goal. They lived in a world of magick and legends, yet Ava's imagination was so limited!

As Minye had explained to Riona, there was a time when men did not exist, and all women possessed magick and lived alongside elves in peace. Then a group of elves, who were keen on unethical experiments, created man and thus began the downfall of woman. Minye further explained that there were no elven men, that humans in general had been an experiment, being created from elven blood and the blood of primates. Once men were created, women lost their power, becoming smaller and weaker over time. The women of Wildoras alone retained their strength, magick, and might, but even they were reduced to nothing with a curse from Azmon, the only man to master magick in all the history of Isliine.

And so, to lift Azmon's curse and to restore to women their magick power, the world needed someone to venture to the ancient resting place of Azmon and there find his talisman and break it. The way Minye had framed it, it had sounded like a simple task to Riona, but she quickly changed her mind on that notion when Minye showed her a map of Isliine: the temple of Azmon was so far away, it was practically at the top of the very world, where snow and ice capped the world's crown. Riona would have to travel very far to reach it, and then she would have to undertake the mighty task of fighting past the guardians of Azmon's temple to reach the talisman.

Minye had insisted it was a task that Riona alone was destined for, that she alone could end the curse over women, and that once the talisman was broken, it would be very easy indeed for Ava to take back Caradin and for all queens the world over to take the throne from their men. Men would dwindle and eventually disappear, and the world would return to its natural state, where women alone would live, thriving in peace.

Once the curse was broken, then – and only then – would the elves return. For, as Minye gently told Riona, it was because they had grown weary of men and their violence that the elves of Elloris had disappeared into the wilderness, never to be seen or heard from again.

Riona wasn't certain she believed much in "destiny" or that she was "the chosen one," but she did want more than anything to help her mother to retake their home, and if it meant restoring power to women without a great deal of bloodshed, then all the better.

With Riona sitting upon her scaly green back, Wulfa flew fast from Erinyel's temple, flew with an urgency that Riona felt in her bones. They had flown often over the temple at night when the others were sleeping, and during that time, Wulfa had been playful, looping in circles across the stars, dipping and rising, and Riona had laughed heartily on her back. But now, Wulfa's wings were heavy and mournful. The dragon did not want to leave the others behind any more than Riona did.

Riona clung to Wulfa's back and thought sadly of Liadan and Ava, Ethne and Lysa, and how they would panic once they had realized she was gone. Sweet Ava would weep, frightened that the Godga would snatch her daughter, and Ethne and Lysa would hotly declare that they should set out immediately and find Riona. Liadan – silent, broody Liadan – would probably sit beside the fire and drink.

They flew all night, speeding against the cool spring air, Riona's long blonde hair whipping back as Wulfa's great tail twisted snakelike against the stars. It was cold, riding at night, and by the time Wulfa had landed the following morning, moisture was clinging to Riona's hair and face. She was grateful to still be wearing her ancient elven armor and the wool underarmor, which had kept her quite warm otherwise.

Tired and aching from the long ride, Riona slid clumsily off Wulfa's back and glanced around. The dragon had landed in a clearing. They were still in Wildhold, of course, surrounded by the enormous moss-covered trees of the endless elven forest. Pale shafts of morning light streamed over them in fingers, and butterflies floated by, birds were singing and flowers blooming in the morning light. Wildhold was so peaceful and beautiful, it sometimes amazed Riona what dangers lurked within it. She had already seen the orcs, and Ethne had told her several stories of giant spiders, wild dragons, and goblins as well. She wondered how much of the Sparrow Knight's stories had been true and hoped they had not been true in the slightest.

"I suppose we can make camp here," said Riona, dropping her bag off her shoulder and glancing around for stones for a fire pit. She started tearing up grass to expose the dirt and was placing stones in a circle when she heard a scream. Riona halted and stood upright again, listening, her hand on her sword hilt. It was a woman screaming.

Wulfa was listening as well. When the scream came again, the dragon nudged Riona in the back with her nose, urging her to look in a certain direction. Riona obeyed and saw the smoke of a fire rising through the trees nearby. They had landed near a camp, and the screams of the distant woman continued.

"Stay here," said Riona. She heard Wulfa snort in protest and added, "I'll whistle if I need you. Dragon hunters are known to come here! I shant let you put yourself at risk needlessly!"

Wulfa snorted again but grudgingly sat on her haunches, angrily slamming her backside down so hard that leaves drifted from the trees. Riona gave the dragon a reproachful look, but Wulfa snorted again, unabashed.

Riona smiled as she turned away. Wulfa was still roughly the size of a bull, though she had grown a little already since their venture from the temple, and Riona wanted to approach the nearby camp unnoticed. Bringing a big dragonling with her was a surefire way to be spotted.

Eyes on the smoke rising through the trees, Riona set off. It didn't take her long to reach the camp. She peered through the bushes and could see what she could only assume were goblins. There were six of them, and the little, bright green men and women were wearing animal skins and hides, were carrying chipped daggers, and had wild, dirty blonde hair. Two of them had bows, but Riona knew she could deflect them easily – that or take out the bowmen first.

Riona could tell the goblins had been camping there for a while. The fire pit looked old, for it was full of much ash, and there were tents made of animal hides nearby that looked ragged with age. There were also bones piled near the fire pit, as if they'd been stripped of flesh. Human bones? Riona shivered in disgust when she saw what might have been a human skull, and her heart skipped a beat when she noticed one of the goblins – a happily humming male in a ragged loincloth – stirring a big pot over the fire. Ethne had said that goblins ate humans, but hearing about it and seeing it were two different things. Actually smelling the cooking flesh was nauseating.

Another scream rose from the camp, and Riona went still when she saw the screaming woman at last: she was an elf! The elven woman was wearing a simple gray traveling gown. She was pale and pretty, with long golden hair falling to her feet and round, frightened blue eyes. Two goblins were hopping circles around her, one ripping and tearing at her traveling gown with his dagger, while the other poked her with his dagger each time she tried to run. A sick feeling rose in the back of Riona's throat: the goblins had eaten the woman's friends and were now preparing to eat her!

"Nummy, nummy!" one of the goblins said, and stopping before the elven woman, he reached up – he and all the goblins were quite short – and ripped the front of her dress open. The elven woman screamed when her breasts shivered free, and they were such beautiful breasts, Riona blushed when she felt herself stirring. They were large and swollen and the pink nipples were so hard. Riona had never seen a woman's breasts that weren't her mother's and felt ashamed when the arousal started pumping between her thighs. This poor woman was in duress, yet she was becoming aroused!

"Focus," Riona muttered to herself.

"Nummy, nummy!" sang the goblin. He reached for the elven woman's breasts with greedy eyes, but she scowled and smacked his long-nailed hands away.

The other goblins laughed heartily.

"Looks like she don't want you, Gor!" chuckled one of the goblin women, whose voice was startlingly shrill. "But what woman would?!"

More laughter from the goblins.

The apparent Gor, seething now that he had been rejected, sneered up at the elven woman and grabbed her sleeve and yanked hard, exposing her shoulder next. The elven woman scowled and – without warning – grabbed her skirt in one small fist, lifted it, and kicked the goblin in the face. As the other goblins squealed with laughter, Gor rolled away through the grass, gnarled feet over his head, his face gushing blood. Furious, he sprang to his feet, grabbed a rock from the ground – and hurled it at the elven woman's shocked face.

Riona tensed in horror, then lunged from the bushes.

ALL TIME SEEMED TO stop as the heavy rock came hurtling at Inara's face. The rock's quick careening slowed to such a crawl that it appeared to be almost floating before her nose. Then it halted completely and dropped harmlessly to the dirt. Clutching her torn gown shut over her breasts, Inara blinked at the heavy rock as it lay at her feet. Just seconds before, it would have crushed into her face and broken her nose. She was on the verge of wondering if she hadn't developed a new power when she heard the goblins screaming and looked up.

Three of the goblins were on fire! They ran circles through the camp, smacking into tents, which set the tents aflame, increasing the chaos, until flames were leaping everywhere. The only goblin who hadn't caught fire was Gor, who was standing in shock, his mouth open, watching as his friends burned alive.

"Ahhhhh! Ahhhhhh!" the screeches echoed through the camp.

Head turning this way and that, Inara watched the goblins and didn't feel at all sorry for them: they had eaten her friends and had been on the verge of eating her! She smiled when she saw how horrified Gor was.

Gor was trembling so badly, his knees were knocking. He fell down to his knees, then folded over and kowtowed, pressing his forehead to the dirt. Wondering who the goblin was bowing to, Inara looked around and her breath caught in her throat: a human woman was marching at a hard swagger through the roaring flames. She was wearing beautiful elven armor, and its silver reflected the flames like water as she came, her messy blonde hair lifting long behind her, her eyes glowing with power. She was tall, and she was muscular, and she was powerful . . . and she was utterly beautiful.

Inara felt herself shaking as the beautiful knight drew near, and she thought she might just fall to her knees and grovel alongside the goblin. She pressed her thighs together to hold herself up and watched as the knight stopped over the goblin. Inara didn't blame the goblin for shaking and cowering: the woman might as well have been six feet tall, a goddess glowing with golden light.

"Please, don't kill me!" the goblin screeched.

Nearby, the other goblins had finally fallen down dead. Their bodies were still gently flaming, as beside them, the ragged tents blazed on. Noticing this, the stranger waved her silver gauntlet almost absently, and the flames evaporated. She did this without turning her fierce blue eyes from the goblin, who cowered before her.

"I was going to eat the missus, yes, but a goblin's gotta eat!" the goblin shrilled, sobbing and weeping quite pathetically, Inara thought.

"You would dare lay your hands on a lady!" sneered the stranger. She was so coldly calm and indignant, but having waved away the flames, her eyes had stopped glowing, and her messy, long hair had stopped floating around her. She no longer looked like a goddess but a terrifying – and yet beautiful – knight. Inara could feel her heart beating in her ears.

"I'm sorry!" the goblin wailed. "Please, let me go! Let me live! I'll never eat another elf again! I swear it on me life!"

To Inara's amazement, the knight stood considering. Her hand was on her sword hilt, as if she might pull it and be done with the goblin. But after some thought, her blue eyes relented, dulling of anger, and she said darkly, "Go. The next day we meet, it shall be your last."

The goblin scrambled to his feet at once. His face was covered in snot and tears, so that Inara almost felt sorry for him. Almost. She hadn't forgotten what he'd done to her friends!

Seeing the fury in Inara's eyes, the goblin gave them both a last frightened glance before turning and scrambling as fast as he could into the trees.

When the goblin had gone, the knight turned to Inara, and her pretty blue eyes were soft with concern. "Are you well, my lady?" she asked, drawing near and looming over Inara, so that she held down a tremble of desire.

Inara's blue eyes grew round in wonder as she gazed up at the big woman. "But . . . who *are* you? A Wildoras woman? A knight? Yet you wear elven armor! The armor of an ancient house, in fact! I've never been so aroused and confused in my entire life."

The knight blushed brightly, and Inara laughed, thinking, *How cute.*

"My name is Riona," said the knight gently, yet confidently, "the third of my name, heir to the throne of Caradin and all of Illa."

Inara's brows went up in disbelief. "You're the princess! The one we came for!"

The towering knight frowned. "What do you mean?"

Inara shook her head apologetically. "That's right. I guess you wouldn't know. You see, one of my f-friends had a vision about you and . . ." Her lip trembled as she tried not to think of Holone, who was the first to be murdered and eaten by the goblins the night before. The woman's screams as Inara was bound and gagged in one of the tents . . . Tears rushed to blind Inara and she bowed her head and sobbed hard. She was trembling all over and so exhausted. The goblins had been holding them for days and hadn't fed them, had enjoyed poking them with sticks and groping them. She suddenly felt as if she would collapse to the ground in tears.

Inara bowed her head and let her pale hair tumble forward, hiding her. She didn't want the knight to see her weep. To her amazement, the knight hesitated, then gently placed a hand on her back and smoothed it down her hair. She had taken off her gauntlet, and the feel of her strong bare hand was so soothing, Inara's sniffles quieted, and she lifted her eyes.

The knight's blue eyes were pitying and kind . . . and warm with something else. Affection? Lust? Inara couldn't tell, but she enjoyed the way the woman looked down at her, as if she wanted to protect her. She even thought there was a moment when the knight wanted to kiss her but was restraining herself. Inara remembered with a blush that her cleavage was rising from her torn dress as she held it shut. She must have been making the poor woman quite uncomfortable.

Inara stepped close and whispered, "Hold me?"

The knight obeyed, closing her arms around Inara, enfolding her in their strength. A flutter of happiness went through Inara's chest, and she smiled, letting her cheek fall against the knight's cold breastplate. But as comforting as the knight's embrace was, the horror of what had happened was still very much with Inara, and she broke down sobbing again.

The knight, in her kindness, stroked Inara's hair again and held her close, humming a soft lullaby. Inara's lashes fluttered in surprise to hear how pleasing the knight's voice was as she hummed. And she was humming something familiar. It was an old elven lullaby. Inara was amazed she even knew it.

Pale lashes fluttering out tears, Inara glanced up and gazed absently at the knight, who gazed down at her with soft-eyed concern. By the gods, she was beautiful, those fierce eyes and all that wild blonde hair. Inara looked at the knight's lips and thinking "Why not?" she rocked up on tiptoe and kissed her warm on the mouth.

Don't miss out!

Visit the website below and you can sign up to receive emails whenever Ash Gray publishes a new book. There's no charge and no obligation.

https://books2read.com/r/B-A-ZRKF-HXEBC

Also by Ash Gray

A Time of Darkness
Time's Arrow
The Infinite Athenaeum

Clan of the Cave Bear
Taken by the Chieftess
Passed Around
Keeping Warm
Her Pretty Pet
Dominated
Seduced
Caught
Savaged

Cyber Mech
Good With Her Hands

Fallen Stars

Fragile Hearts
Broken Minds
Digital Heartbeats
Electric Souls
Metal Bones

Her First Knight
The Knight of the Wild
Sparrow Song
Rowan's Hammer
The Dragon of Almara
Sanctuary
The Flower of Adwean
The Halls of Erinyel
The Daughter of Light
The Tomb of Azmon
Queen Liadan

Knight of Fire
The Queen of Swords
The Three of Goblets
The Queen of Wands
The Queen of Goblets
The Star
The World

Knights of Passion
The Queen's Lust

Handfasting the Warrior Queen
The Revenge of Raven's Cross
The Light of Lythara
Taming the Wolf Knight
The Mermaids of Menosea
The Fairy Queen of Elwenhal
The Dragon of Edhen
Essential Selene
Hearth and Home
Aereth's Return
The Fairy Ring
The Main Course
Knights of Passion: The Complete Series

Knights of Vallor
Saving Salia
Raven Spirit
Eryet's Fountain
The Daughter of Idet
The Mirror of Iovar
Aine's Athenaeum
Bone and Fire
Princess Eydis

Ona of Ozmora
The Amulet of Tizra
The Bandit Queen of Crystal Falls
The Council of Eldor
The Sword of Avara
Wicked Things in the Wilds

Pirates of Artusa
Stolen Booty
Taking Her Sword
Marooned

Tales of the Blood Moon Coven
Bloodlust
The Hidden Memory
Whispered Names
Morbid Fascination
Bending to Her Will
Blood Rage
Prey
Hunted
Voyeuristic Intentions
Interludes and Ecstasy

The Assassin's Kiss
Crossed Daggers
Swordplay

The Chronicles of Omicron
The Thieves of Nottica
The Watchtower of Rustoria

The Dragon Riders of Valheera
Birthday Surprises

The Dreamscape
Out of Mind
Recalling Color

The Last Queen of Qorlec
Project Mothership
The Harvest
The Suns of Anarchy
The Light-year Lion
Moon Fire
Exiled Stars
Zora's Stone

The Legend of Kiva
The Starlight Stair

The Pussycat Chronicles
The Heist
Broken Hearts and Brain Damage
Candy, Sweat, and Regret
Lip Gloss and Loose Women

Witch Xim
Rezzora's Workshop

Standalone
Qorth
Fall Apart World
Unicorn Blood

About the Author

Ash Gray is a lesbian living in California. She writes lesfic (aka fiction for lesbians) in science fiction, fantasy, and paranormal settings.